My Heart Weeps

Pamela S Thibodeaux

"For I know the plans I have for you," declares the Lord, "plans to prosper you and not to harm you, plans to give you hope and a future."

~ Jeremiah 29:11 NIV

My Heart Weeps
by
Pamela S Thibodeaux

Publisher/Distributor:
Temperance Publishing; an imprint of
Pamela S. Thibodeaux Enterprises, LLC
PO Box 324
Iowa, LA 70647

Cover Design: Tania @ Get Covers

Published in the Unites States of America
Publishing History: First edition August 18th, 2020

Praise for My Heart Weeps

"Pamela Thibodeaux uses her masterful story writing art to create a powerful story of how God heals a woman's heart —broken by grief— through recovery, love and triumph." ~ CBA Best-Selling Author DiAnn Mills

"My heart wept along with Melena's in this wonderful story of loss, heartbreak, healing and renewal. Pamela S. Thibodeaux is a gifted author with a talent for touching the emotional core of her readers. Be prepared for tears. Expect laughter. Enjoy the experience." ~ Delia Latham, Inspirational Romance Author

*"**My Heart Weeps** is a compelling, emotional novel about grieving widow Melena, who is struggling to recover from her husband's death. Ms. Thibodeaux perfectly evokes the pain Melena endures and then brings us a ray of light and hope when Melena gets a second chance at love. A heartwarming must-read."* ~ Author Alicia Dean

*"**My Heart Weeps**, beautifully written, you feel the pain, heartache, and loss, right alongside Melena. If you have experienced life's painful surprises, or horrible crisis's and wished you'd never encountered such misery, hang on! You can find a renewed spirit ... as Author Pamela S. Thibodeaux takes you on a heartfelt journey of recovery, hope, and triumph!"* ~ Minority Women Business

Enterprise owner, (MWBE) Multiple Award-Winning Author, Linda J. Hawkins

*"Partly based on the author's own personal experience of losing her husband, **My Heart Weeps** is a touching story of overcoming grief. It appeals to all human beings who must come to terms with the death of a loved one. This novel offers a positive, uplifting experience."* ~ Author, Jacqueline Seewald

Praise for Pamela S. Thibodeaux

"A great collection of short stories. Each one includes inspirational romance. Wonderful choice when you need a quick pick-me-up. I have not been one to read short stories. This book has changed that. There are times when they are the perfect choice." ~ (Amazon) Review of **Love in Season** by K. Neely

"Loved this book. Wish everyone could read this. Definitely puts all holidays in perspective. If we remember the reason for the holidays then we must put God first.......always. I will certainly recommend this book. Great stuff keep up the great writing." ~ (Amazon) Review of **Keri's Christmas Wish** by Reba

"Oh, the passion, faith and just LIFE that flows through this book...powerful writing indeed!" ~ Review of **Circles of Fate** by Deena Peterson, Book Reviewer @ A Peek at my Bookshelf and Just One More

"Thibodeaux leads the reader through from the first page to the last without once relinquishing control. She hooks them, holds them, and keeps them enthralled until the last line." ~ Review of **The Visionary** by Delia Latham, author of the "Solomon's Gate" series

*"**In His Sight** caught my attention from the beginning and it made me wonder if I had given all to God as he gave all to me. Thank*

you, Pamela, for a story that I would readily recommend to anyone who needs that extra encouragement!" ~ Reviewed by Wendy for Happily Ever After Reviews *Part of **Love in Season** collection of short stories*

*"**Winter Madness** is a wonderful romance and an excellent example of Spiritual growth."* ~Reviewed by Dee Daily for The Romance Studio *Part of **Love in Season** collection of short stories*

*"**A Hero for Jessica** is a good, sweet read charged with attraction but an emphasis on true love. I recommend it to women of all ages."* ~ Reviewed by Violet for LASR *Part of **Love in Season** collection of short stories*

*"**Cathy's Angel** is a short tale that is entertaining as well as inspiring. Well done!"* ~ Reviewed by Marlene for Fallen Angel Reviews *Part of **Love in Season** collection of short stories*

"Pamela S. Thibodeaux's motto is "Inspirational with an Edge! ™" Her short story **Choices** lives up to those words and is well worth reading."* ~ Reviewed by Gail for Night Owl Romance *Part of **Love in Season** collection of short stories*

*"**The Inheritance** was my first Thibodeaux work; however, it will not be my last! Her approach to writing about everyday life, while struggling to maintain strict Christian standards and values,*

is a glimpse into reality which we all must face from time to time.”
~ Reviewed by Brenda Talley for The Romance Studio

*“If you have ever considered Christian fiction bland, then check out the **Tempered Series.** It will be well worth your time.”* ~ Amanda Killgore for Huntress Reviews

*“**Lori’s Redemption** is fast paced, lots of action, gripping storyline... I loved it. It's gone straight back into my TBR pile.”* ~ Clare Revell author of the “Monday’s Child” series

“Through Pamela's blessed ability to find God everywhere, even in secular song lyrics, she has written devotions guaranteed to touch the heart and remind the reader of our True Love, the Rose of Sharon.” ~ Endorsement for **Love is a Rose** by Linda Yezak, Author

Dedication

To everyone who has survived the loss of a loved one and journeyed through the grieving process to come out stronger, better, wiser, healed, whole, complete, **OR**, in the very least, at peace – this book is for you.

To my family who travelled this road with me.... TJ, Karol, Bryan, Monica, Mark, Bubba, Bryanna, Sean, Karson, my Parents, Brothers and extended family – THANK YOU! I could not– would not – be here today were it not for the love, support and concern you expressed during the darkest time in my life.

To ALL the friends in my life who helped me through the transition from wife to widow to individual – there are too many of you to mention but I'll name a few... Pat, Jerrie, Nona, Salena, Paulia, Julie, Jillian, Randy, Mitzi & Frank, BWG Friends – Please know, Pat Green is a reflection of what you ALL were/are to me – I love Each of You and Thank You from the bottom of my heart for the blessing you were and continue to be in my life!

To the wonderful people who worked with me at the Silver Spur Guest Ranch and my other Bandera peeps .... Kay & Garry, Maybelle, Lishelle & Matt, Penny & Smitty, Patti, Allison, Robert, Ricochet, David, Jay, Maria, Denise and so many more! – You were the wind beneath my wings back then. Your love and support were unsurpassed, and it is partly because of YOU that I'm the woman I am today.

If I have left anyone out of these lists, please know it was NOT intentional and that I DO love and appreciate every person who was, is or has been a part of this journey that is my life ~ May God Bless Each and Every One of YOU with a rich increase of HIS almighty good!

Chapter One

Melena Rhyker stood in silence as the line of attendees passed by with whispered words of encouragement and condolence. She pressed a fist to her mouth to keep the scream from escaping and fought the urge to cover her ears.

My life is over. How am I to survive? Why should I? I don't care what others say, their words are empty, meaningless. I want it to be over. I've no reason to live anymore. I wish these people would just shut up and leave me alone! I can't do this. I want to go home.

Pictures flashed through her head...the kids, grandbabies, parents, and siblings...all those reasons to hang on.

So much to do. So many decisions to make.

Lord, give me strength.

The cold mahogany casket housing her husband's body mocked the faith she'd clung to throughout his brief, devastating illness.

She heard Satan snicker.

Melena swallowed the hot surge of bile in her throat.

"Mom?" Her son's voice and his hand on her waist pulled her into the moment. "It's time to go."

Melena shook her head and placed trembling fingers over her lips. Tears filled her eyes, spilled over. "I can't."

Jon Jr. took her hands and pulled her into a hug. "We have to, Mom. People are already gathering at the house."

"Tell them to go somewhere else." She raised wide eyes to his. Panic sluiced through her. "I can't do this, Jon. I don't want to." Her knees threatened to buckle. She clung to her son, rubbing a palm over her chest. "It hurts!"

He wrapped his arms around her, buried his face in her hair and swallowed hard. "I know, Mom. I know," he mumbled, his tone grief-stricken and raw. "But we have to do our best. Dad would expect that. One day at a time. Come on, now."

Melena surrendered as her daughter stepped up beside her, placed an arm around her waist, and aided Jon in leading her out of the mausoleum and into the waiting car.

Hours later, she sat alone in the house where she'd shared most of her life and all of her heart with her husband, her friend, her lover.

The father of her children.

Panic rose. She stumbled to the sink and threw up every crumb she'd choked down that day.

Oh God, what am I going to do?

For the first time in her long walk of faith, she feared God had forsaken her.

She splashed cold water on her face and neck, grabbed the dishtowel and patted herself dry. A memory rose of the many times she'd chided Jon for wiping his face with her clean dish towel.

"I'm sorry for all the petty grievances, Jon. I'll never nag you again. Just come back." She didn't resist when her knees crumpled, but sprawled out on the kitchen floor, buried her face in the cloth and wept.

* * * * *

Melena awoke in a tangle of sheets and sweat. Sun streamed through her window. Birds chirped. The sights and sounds of life all around did little to revive her spirit. On automatic pilot, her body demanded coffee so she stumbled into the kitchen, rinsed the burned on, day-old liquid from the pot, and measured out grounds. Pain throbbed through her when she realized there was no need to make a full one. Her hand trembled. Water dribbled onto the counter. She bit the inside of her cheek to keep from crying out, dumped coffee grounds back into the canister and started over. She pressed the ON button and stared out the window.

How can everything appear so normal when my whole world has fallen apart?

When the coffee finished brewing, she poured herself a cup and sat at the table. The phone rang. Caller ID showed her employer's number.

She sipped, tempted to ignore the call but the insistent ringing wouldn't let her. She picked up the receiver. "I can't come in today."

"It's been two weeks, Melena. I need you. The company needs you. Your coworkers are worried. No one is complaining, mind you, but everyone is concerned. You need to get back to normal."

"I've no idea what normal is anymore," Melena admitted. "I'm sorry, Bruce. We'll see how I feel tomorrow."

Five minutes later, her son called and seconded her boss's sentiments. "Why don't you try to go in for a couple of hours, or half the day? You've got to start somewhere. Staying stuck in that house can't be good for you."

"I don't stay stuck in the house. I go to the cemetery every day."

"You can still go to the cemetery, Mom, if you feel you need to, but get back into your routine. It'll help."

Melena sighed. "Maybe tomorrow." She hung up before he could say another word. When the phone rang again—her daughter this time—she let the answering machine pick it up. She pushed the half-empty cup away and buried her face on her arm. *Two weeks?* Her head throbbed. Pain lanced through her entire body. *How on earth have I made it two weeks?* She massaged the spot in her chest where the ache throbbed with every beat of her pulse. "It hurts!"

The cry reverberated through the empty room, echoed in her soul. The numbness lifted, replaced by pain...deep, raw, agonizing. Everything was done, finalized. Nothing to think about. No plans to make. No decisions to wade through. Melena had no idea what to think, how to feel, or even what to pray anymore.

I just want to go home...Jesus, please just take me home.

* * * * *

Melena struggled awake through a mild state of panic to find herself on the floor beside her bed. She pulled herself to her knees, and then to her feet. Another day had dawned, another week passed, and for some reason, God hadn't seen fit to take her home as she'd asked—no, as she'd pleaded and begged Him to. And not for the first time either.

She raised her eyes toward the ceiling. "Why, Lord? There's got to be a reason I'm still here, but what is it? I'm so torn, so unsettled. I hate this! If this pain doesn't kill me, the job will. I hate my life and everything about it...the monotony...get up, go to work, smile and pretend to be okay when I'm dying inside. Then I come home to this empty house. Empty bed. Oh God, how am I going to do this? Why should I?"

She pulled her journal out of the bedside table drawer and continued her conversation with God....

I roll up my feelings like a sleeping bag and stuff them away for the next eight hours. Please God, let no one ask how I'm doing. If they do, I'm going to go off on them and it's not going to be pretty. They'll probably haul me off in a straitjacket, kicking and screaming all the way—Then again, three or four days in a padded cell just might be what I need to sort all this out in my mind. In my heart— what's left of it anyway. Oh, the muscle is there and perfectly healthy—damn it!—pumping blood through my body as it should. Funny how it can still function when I buried it three weeks ago. Why, God? I don't understand! Why did you take him? How am I ever going to get through this?

One day at a time.

The answer echoes through my soul but brings little relief. Everyone—kids, parents, well-meaning friends—say I should see a doctor, maybe get on some kind of anti-depressant or something, but I don't want to do that. Been there, done that and I'm not going back to that place...the deep, dark, pit of apathy.

I'd rather hurt than feel nothing at all.

God, help me hang on without the need for drugs.

Melena put the journal away, took a shower, and dressed for work. A gloomy fog marred the Mississippi morning, mirroring her mood. She added a sweater to her wardrobe and left the house early enough to stop by the cemetery, where she found a measure of peace to continue the day. At 6 p.m., she pulled into the carport, turned off the engine and laid her head on the steering wheel.

"Well, I'm home again. Made it through another agonizing eight hours or so, now to get through another night."

Gathering every ounce of courage she could summon, she disembarked from her vehicle, retrieved the mail from the box beside the door, and entered the house. She thumbed through the envelopes and advertisements, then laid them on the table and poured a glass of juice. She reached for the bottle of over-the-counter pain reliever and froze.

It would be so easy to end this pain.

Oh, what an enticing thought. Just take a handful of pills and end it all. Would she wake up in heaven? Would Jesus meet her there? Would Jonathan? What about the kids or Mama—would they understand? Or would she destroy them? Where was the faith she claimed to have? Why was it failing her now?

I can't do this!

More importantly, she didn't want to.

She pushed the bottle away, drank the juice and escaped into a hot bath. The warm water and bath salts soothed her tangled emotions. When the temperature cooled, she rose from the tub, performed her nightly toiletries and eased into bed.

Several hours later, she awoke, startled and disoriented. She sat up, drew her knees to her chest and rested her cheek a moment. She took Jon's picture off the table, caressed the beloved image. "Guess I ought to get up off the floor and into the bed. Not the first time I woke up in a fetal position on this filthy rug. Not even sure how I get here each time."

She'd talked to him every day the last thirty years of her life and had no qualms about talking to him now. Far sight better than talking to herself.

Maybe.

She swallowed convulsively and stroked his face, his smile, his eyes. "I dreamed of you again. You were so alive and healthy. Radiant. Oh, God..." The words trembled on a sob. "How I wish it were so."

She longed to touch him; to trace his moustache, run her fingers through his hair...press her lips to his. Her arms ached to hold him close. Why is it he appeared so full of life when she'd watched him die? Day after day, she'd watched the strong, beautiful man wither away into a mere shell, and in one moment, with one final gasp of breath, his life was over.

"I visit you daily, yet everything seems so surreal. Like I'm walking through a dream." She shoved the picture back onto the table, bit her lip and nearly choked on the hard knot of anger in her throat. "No, not a dream. Dreams are wonderful, full of hope and magic. This is a nightmare."

Would she ever wake? Would she ever be whole again? Or would she wade through life only half alive?

The alarm screamed in her ear. Bright red numbers flashed 6:30 a.m. on the display. Melena slapped it off then dragged herself off the floor, stumbled into the bathroom and stared at the ghastly sight in the mirror. Her eyes were puffy and swollen, nose red, stuffy and congested. "I can't go to work like this. I look like hell, and worse, I feel as bad as I look."

She bowed her head and chanted the mantra that had gotten her through the past several weeks. "I don't understand, Lord, but I trust

You."

Despite the effort, thoughts whirled in her head...*Feels like a lie. How can I trust Him when He took the very reason I lived and breathed? Jonathan was my whole life. My world revolved around him, and now he's gone. We so looked forward to this time in our marriage—when the kids are all grown and gone, time for just us. We planned and dreamed of these days for so long and now...now the dreams are shattered along with every hope we had for the future. I don't know what to do, where to go, what to say, how to feel. Half the time I'm numb and the other half, I wish I was. A drink would be nice, but I'm afraid I won't stop at just one. Besides, it's too early in the morning.*

It's five o'clock somewhere.

Oh yeah.

* * * * *

Melena squinted at the clock through eyes blurry from lack of sleep and swollen from too much crying. 11:30 a.m. The phone rang and the sound reverberated through her skull. She picked it up.

"Mom, are you all right?" Her daughter's voice echoed over the line.

"Don't know if I'll ever be all right again."

"Are you sick? You sound strange."

"No, I'm not sick. Drunk, but not sick." The contents of her stomach started to sour and churn. "Not yet anyway."

"Drunk? You never drink!"

The shock in her child's voice made her giggle, and then groan. She rested her forehead in her palm. "Your father and I enjoy a glass of wine now and then."

"Well, Bruce called and said you sounded pretty bad when you left a message that you wouldn't be in, so I thought I'd check on you."

"Maybe I'll get lucky, and he'll fire me."

Kathryn gasped. "Don't say that, Mom. You've always loved your job. Things will get better. Get some rest today and try again tomorrow. That's all we can do. Besides, you know Dad wouldn't want to see you like this."

"Then he shouldn't have left me here by myself." Melena slammed the receiver into its cradle. Ten minutes later, after a call from her son and a subsequent one from her mother, she turned the ringer off.

The next afternoon she greeted the entire family when they knocked on her door with their pastor in tow.

Pastor Jim stepped around her son and took her hand in his. "How are you, Melena?"

Melena turned and led the entourage into the kitchen. "Well, I survived my foray into alcoholic bliss. Not that there was much bliss if you count the headache, vomiting and smelling like a derelict."

"But did it help?" Her son asked.

She shook her head, took deep breaths and blinked fast to stem the deluge. "No. Nothing's changed. The pain is still there. But guess you all knew that, which is why you're here."

Her father enfolded her against his chest. "No one is here to judge you, honey, or fuss. We just want you to know how much we care and that we are here for you."

Melena rested in his embrace a moment. "Thank you, Daddy." She gave him a fierce hug, and then turned toward the counter. "Coffee, anyone?"

Everyone sat at the table while she and her mother prepared the coffee and set out cups and saucers. As they sipped in strained silence, her daughter moved to speak. Melena held up a hand. "I know you are all worried, but some way, somehow, I'll get through this."

Pastor Jim placed a hand over hers. "One day, one moment, one prayer at a time, Melena. That's all any of us can do. But please know counseling is available if you feel the need for it. With me, or I can refer you to another pastor, a grief counselor, or a support group. Whatever it takes. There is no shame in it either."

Melena's lips trembled into a tiny smile. "Thank you." Her gaze swept the table to encompass those who loved her. "Thank you all, but I have to do this on my own."

"That's just it, Mom, you don't *have* to do it alone," Jon inserted.

"Yes, I do. Everyone grieves in his or her own way. I know you are all hurting too. I don't know how to help, and I certainly don't want to burden you with my grief. I know you're here for me and I know you care and are worried. I feel the same toward each of you. But grief is very personal and each of us has to find his or her own way through it. It's only been a few weeks but if I don't start feeling better, if things don't settle some and if I truly feel like I need help, medical or otherwise, I'll get it. That's a promise."

Chapter Two

Melena's hand trembled as she touched the date etched in stone. *You've stopped counting the weeks, but it's been three months today.* The thought slammed into her, brought her to her knees. A flood of moisture blinded her. Her chest tightened with the effort to get air in and out of her lungs. She heard a keening wail, not realizing it came from her own lips.

"Ma'am?" Strong hands pulled her to her feet.

"H—he's—g—gone. He's—n—never—c—coming back."

"I'm so sorry. Can I call someone for you?"

She shook her head then gazed up at the gentleman, noticing the somber attire and collar which indicated he was a clergyman. "I don't know how I'm going to get through this. My children and parents think it'll get easier with time, but it's been three months. Some days I'm fairly okay, and then BAM!" She pounded a fist against her chest. "It hits me like a freight train."

He patted her hand and led her to a bench nearby then handed her his handkerchief. "What type of grief coping mechanisms have you tried?"

"I pray and meditate, and I journal. I haven't written anything lately though because it doesn't seem to help. Nothing's changed. This ache is constant—sometimes like a throbbing tooth, others like a thousand sharp knives shredding me to ribbons." She dabbed her eyes. "I'm sorry. I'm probably keeping you from whatever you came here for."

He glanced at his watch. "I have a few more minutes. You sure I can't call someone, one of your children maybe or your parents?"

"I need to call my boss. He'll probably get all bent out of shape again with worry, but I can't go in today. Not like this."

He pulled a cell phone out of his pocket. "Let me do that for you."

Melena agreed and punched her work number into the device and hit the call button. She fought down another wave of hysteria while the minister explained how and where he'd found her and that she was okay but wouldn't be in to work today.

He ended the call, closed the phone and slid it into his pocket. "He said he'll see you tomorrow and to take care. Are you okay to drive home?"

She stood and extended her hand to him. "Yes. Thank you so much. I guess what they say about talking to strangers in lieu of loved ones is true."

He squeezed her hand then gave her a business card. "Sometimes it's easier to unload your burden with someone who isn't personally affected by the circumstances. Feel free to call me anytime."

Melena acknowledged the invitation with a slight nod then walked to her car. She started the engine then sat a minute, gaining a measure of calm, and sent up a silent prayer of thanks for the angel God had sent to intervene in her bout of insanity. After she arrived home and answered calls from both of her children as well as parents, she sat in the den with her journal and recorded the incident.

I still can't seem to wrap my mind around the idea that Jon will never come home. I'll never see his face or hear his voice. His arms will not reach for me in the night or any time for that matter. I don't know how to do this—keep going, keep living—or even if I want to.

She put the diary away, but her thoughts continued to whirl as the reality that she had to make a change in her life sank deeper into her spirit. "But what?" she wondered aloud. "Aside from ending the misery, what can I do?"

The next morning, she crawled from beneath the covers and made the bed as she had the past thirty years of her life. *The monotony is killing me.* Every nerve in her body stood on end with the thought. She jerked the bedding back, fluffed the pillows and tossed them carelessly onto the mattress then walked into the kitchen where the coffee sat, perfectly brewed.

Half a pot.

Damnit!

The quick spurt of anger blinded in its intensity. She slammed the pot into the sink then sucked in a sharp breath as a piece of splintered glass pierced her palm. She wrapped a clean dishcloth around the cut to stem the bleeding, poured a glass of juice and sat at the table. The phone rang.

"Hello?"

"Hi, Mel, it's Pat."

Her spirits lifted a little at the sound of her best friend's voice. "Hey, Pat. Are you home or off on another mission to save the world?"

Pat laughed, a joyful, carefree sound that grated on Melena's last nerve.

"I'm home. How are you, Jon and the kids?"

Melena glanced down. Her hand throbbed in cadence with the cringe of her heart and seeped fresh blood into the towel. She pressed her fingers into a tight fist and swallowed hard. "Jon died three months ago. I tried to reach you but couldn't."

Pat's gasp said more than words could express. "I'll be there in five."

Melena hung up, took a sip of juice then laid her head on the table. Her closest friend, one she'd known since childhood, the one person she'd always counted on to be there when she needed a shoulder or an ear, was on her way. Like a knight in shining armor or an angel sent straight from heaven. She didn't bother to stem the torrent of emotions or bury the grief when, in less than five minutes, Pat stood on her step. She simply opened the door and collapsed into a sobbing heap in her best friend's arms.

Pat held on tight as they slid to the floor, then rocked Melena as she would a child. "What happened, Mel? When I left six months ago everyone and everything was fine."

Before she could answer, Pat took Melena's injured hand in hers and unwrapped it. "Let's get this cut cleaned up and then you can tell me what happened."

Unable to speak for the sobs still shaking her, Melena nodded and let Pat help her to her feet and into the bathroom. Within minutes she found herself seated at the kitchen table once more, her hand bandaged, and the mess cleaned up. Pat found the spare carafe Melena had stored in the pantry and brewed a fresh pot. Once the coffee finished and cups were prepared, she pulled a chair out across from her and sat down. She took Melena's hand in hers once more and again asked what happened to Jon.

Melena's hand trembled when she lifted the cup to her lips and took a sip of the scalding liquid. "Some kind of blood infection, similar to leukemia only quicker and more vicious. He was gone before we had a chance to really deal with it. Funny, but I can't remember the name of the culprit that took my husband's life. You'd think it'd be etched in my memory forever."

Having been a registered nurse for over twenty years, Pat would know or have a pretty good idea of what the disease was.

"There are a few that fit the description. The mind has a way of blocking things in times like these. You may remember at some point. Doesn't matter though. How are you holding up?"

Melena shook her head, reached for a tissue and buried her face in her hand until the torrent of anguish passed. "Not too well. Everything is such a mess. Everyone thinks I should just get back into my normal routine, but I can't seem to get on stable ground again. The holidays are a blur. Don't know how any of us made it through, but we did. The babies seem blissfully unaware of the pain we adults can't seem to rid ourselves of—even for a moment, much less an entire day."

"Oh, the joy of youth," Pat interjected. Melena's smile wavered but she tried. Conversation stopped when she pushed back from the table and retrieved the pot to refill their cups. Once seated again, she continued—

"Karyn, being the oldest grandchild, hurts the most from missing her "Pops," but seems to be doing well. Most of the time anyway. Kathryn says Karyn has nightmares, cries a lot and doesn't want to go to school. Kathryn can't even go a whole day without breaking down. Chris is at his wits end with the both of them, but I gotta hand it to my son-in-law, he's a real trouper despite his own grief. You know his background and that he came from a broken home."

"Yeah, Jon was his idol, his hero."

Melena nodded. "I don't know how to help them or what to say. Pray, I tell them, but it feels so pat, like such an empty promise." She woofed out a sigh, sipped her coffee. "I've begun to hate my job, to despise the day-in and day-out drudgery. To say I need a change of pace, a change of scenery is an understatement, but I don't know what to do with the rest of my life. All I know is that I can't keep going in the same rut I've been in. Before Jonathan died, the rut had meaning and purpose. Now my life has neither."

"Maybe you should take some time off, a sabbatical or extended leave of absence and travel or something."

Melena smiled at the suggestion. "That's your style, not mine."

Pat had the grace to laugh. "Yeah, wanderlust has plagued my soul since the day I entered into this world." She reached for Melena's hand. "I'm sorry I wasn't here. You know I'd have taken the first plane home had I known he was sick."

Melena squeezed her friend's hand but shook her head. "He wouldn't have wanted that. I'd read your letters and postcards to him and we always got a kick out of dreaming that one day we'd do something as carefree and as meaningful as what you do every day of your life."

"What you two did here, raising such wonderful kids and being pillars of this community is every bit as meaningful as the medical missions I go on. Don't you ever doubt that or look back with regrets."

"Oh, I don't. All I've ever wanted out of life was to be a wife and mother. Now that that is no longer part of the plan, I have no idea what God wants me to do."

The phone rang. Melena glanced at caller ID and sighed. "It's Jon. Every time I don't go to work—which is a lot lately—Bruce calls one of the kids or mom and dad and the phone goes ballistic."

"That's what you get for being the man's Administrative Assistant for twenty-plus years." Pat answered the phone before the machine could pick up. "Rhyker residence, Pat Greene speaking."

She hummed and nodded at whatever Jon said.

"That she is, sweet boy. And how are you?"

More hums and nods, then, "Best any of us can do. I'll have your mom call you later tonight." A pause.

"Not a problem. You're very welcome," Pat said, and Melena knew Jon, ever the polite one, was expressing his gratitude at having 'Aunt Pat' home again.

Pat hung up, sipped her coffee and addressed Melena again. "What do you say we get out of the house? Go shopping or something— whatever you want to do."

What I want *to do is curl up and die.* "Okay."

Pat rose, pulled Melena out of her chair and urged her into the shower. "I'll pick out your clothes and we'll spend the day out on the town."

After visiting the cemetery and grabbing a fruit and juice smoothie, Pat determined a little retail therapy was in order. Hours later they sat together over a late lunch/early supper.

"Well, I must say you definitely look better with a little color in your face."

Melena sighed. "Thank you. I'd forgotten how much fun we used to have when we spent the day together."

"So did all this frivolous energy give you any ideas about the future? There's a light in your eyes that wasn't there this morning."

Melena smiled. "You always could look right into my soul. Actually, I'm thinking I should take your advice and quit my job or take an extended leave of absence."

"I think that's a great idea. Have you put numbers together with your finances to see how long you could go without a regular income?"

"Only in my head, but I think I have enough for the better part of this year."

"What will you do? I mean, staying holed up in the house is definitely not healthy."

Melena leaned back in her chair with a sigh. "It's never easy, is it? I mean, I get all excited about finally making a decision for myself, and up pops a dozen other issues to consider."

She thought a moment, shrugged. "Maybe I'll work on my art. Jon always said I have talent and that I should do something with it. But I've been content to use it only as a means to gift others. Maybe if I put as much passion and energy into painting and glasswork as I did my marriage, our home, and our life together, I could be successful enough to earn a decent living." She blew out a breath. "I don't know...I can't think past tomorrow or next week, much less the future. It's all so overwhelming."

"You could always come with me when I leave again in a couple of months."

Melena smiled. "There's a thought. My savings won't last forever, but if I can take the remainder of this year off, maybe I can back up and regroup, then figure out what's next."

"Well, I think it's a marvelous idea and don't let anyone talk you out of it. Now how about we find a movie or something?"

Melena rolled her shoulders. "To be honest, I'm pretty tired. Haven't expended this much good energy in months. Can we take a rain check?"

"Of course." Pat reached for Melena's lunch ticket and gave the waiter both slips and a credit card. "My treat."

When the young man walked away to take care of her transaction, she leaned over and put a hand over Melena's. "I just want to say one thing before we leave and I drop you off. Despite how well I know you, I have no idea what you're going through, so I won't try to console you with empty phrases or meaningless words. I'm not going to even attempt to make decisions for you either, but I will say this much...if you don't change the status quo, you're not going to make it through this."

Melena's breath hitched on a sob. "I know, but I have no idea what to do."

"I can't solve that dilemma for you, Mel, but my advice is to take some time for yourself, whether it's a month or a year, and let God lead you. He'll show you the way."

* * * * *

Two weeks later Melena sat piled up in bed with Jon's picture. She'd quit her job and the family was in an uproar, afraid she'd close herself off like a hermit and go quietly insane or worse, waste away.

If only it were that easy.

Only Pat seemed to understand this gnawing uncertainty she felt, this need to pack up and run. Go somewhere. Do something. Anywhere. Anything. But what and where? Maybe without the job hanging over her head, she could figure out the answer to at least this one question.

A house divided will fall.

"Well, we're divided and falling apart."

Would they ever be whole again?

"God, give them the comfort I can't."

* * * * *

The phone rang, jerking Melena out of a sound sleep. "Hello?"

"Melena, it's Debbie."

She struggled to wake and clear her mind. She'd been home a month now and still wasn't sure if quitting had been the right decision. Especially since her boss or his new assistant called on a regular basis to check up on her, or get instructions on how to do something she'd handled for him for more than twenty years. But she enjoyed the freedom to come and go as she pleased and not be stuck behind a desk all day. She listened to the current dilemma and offered suggestions.

"It's been five months today. How are you doing? Really?"

The question surprised her. She and Debbie had worked together only a short while before Jon died so she didn't really know the woman on an intimate level. Her constantly raw emotions, however, prevented her from anything less than blatant honesty. "I'm still breathing, still eating." *Sometimes.* "Still functioning." *Somewhat.*

"Not really living, but not quite dead."

She paused to get a handle on her thoughts and cleared her throat to break the awkward silence that sprang up between them. "I'm losing weight, which isn't all bad. I admit this isn't the healthiest way to do so, although I am walking daily, sometimes twice a day."

"Bet it feels good to be out in the sunshine, when there is sunshine." A trace of melancholy colored Debbie's tone. "This winter has been so cold, so nasty."

"Yeah, but I relish the few hours a day of relative warmth and look forward to getting outside. Still not sure what the future holds and still overwhelmed when I try to think or plan too far ahead but I've been spending a lot more time in prayer. That helps too." *Somewhat.*

"Sounds like you're doing okay then. Getting any artwork done? That is why you quit, right...to pursue your craft?"

Melena stifled a yawn. "Sort of. Haven't done anything new but I have started exploring my options, searching the Internet for inspiration and direction. I've set up a website and dug out a couple pieces of art and sold them online. I've also written half a dozen art-related articles for which I received a whopping fifteen-dollars each." She let out a rueful little laugh, surprised when Debbie chuckled too.

"Hey, it all adds up. Right?"

Who knows? It's all so exhausting. Melena skipped an answer and simply hummed in agreement. They talked a few more minutes, and then Debbie thanked her for the help and rang off.

Chapter Three

Melena paced the house, the cordless phone clamped tight against her ear. "Oh, wow, Pat, guess what just popped up in my email? A grant for residency at an artist's retreat! For the first time since Jon's illness, I feel a sense of excitement. The grant only covers two weeks of residency, but somehow it just feels right. I can hardly imagine it. I mean, two weeks of peace and quiet and inspiration, two weeks someplace totally different from here! I've never applied for a grant and the deadline is midnight." Panic tightened her chest. "I don't know what I'm doing."

Delayed by distance, Pat's voice echoed over the line. "Go for it, girl!" Then she was gone as the cell service dropped the call.

Melena replaced the phone in its cradle, sat at the computer and read the grant submission guidelines again. The personal information was easy—*name, address, employment status, etc.*—but when it came to the one-page essay as to why she wanted to attend the retreat, Melena's thoughts screeched to a halt. Overwhelmed, she pushed back the chair and fell to her knees. "Oh, Lord, give me the words...if this is even remotely Your will, help me."

Peace enveloped her. She scrambled into the chair, closed her eyes and typed.

Hours later she lay in bed, wide awake, her thoughts in turmoil. She sat up and tried to pray, but the whirlwind in her brain wouldn't stop, so she did what she always had. Hugging his pillow, she picked up his photo and talked to Jon. "Well, the grant application is gone. I emailed it moments ago and received my confirmation. The recipients will be notified on April 30th and residency can be taken at any time between May and July. I could even split it up into two separate weeks. It's in God's hands but...well, tomorrow I'm going to research the retreat center and see if I can afford a week or two there just in case I don't get the grant. I'm so wound up I can't sleep. Maybe I'll research that place now...."

She put the pillow down, carried his picture with her into the kitchen and brewed a pot of coffee. They went into the office. Melena sat down at the computer and re-read the advertisement for the grant.

Find the inspiration you need to create brilliant artwork at the Crossed Penn Ranch, Utopia, TX.

A few keystrokes and she had the retreat's website pulled up. Her breath escaped in an awed gasp. The phone rang and she all but jumped out of her skin. "Hello?"

Pat's voice came over the line, much clearer than earlier. "Hey girlfriend, did you get that grant application off?"

"Yes, and now I can't sleep. I'm sitting here like a goofy-eyed teenager mooning over a rock star." She giggled. "You should see this place! It's stunning. Their logo is two feather-plumed pens in the shape of a cross. It's in Utopia, TX."

"Wow, what an apt name for the location of an artist's retreat."

"Yeah," Melena agreed. "Utopia, in the Texas Hill Country. Who would have guessed Texas housed such lovely hills? The prices are a bit steep—"

"Don't go there, girl." Pat interrupted. "This is in God's hands. He promises us hope and a future."

"I know that, but right now I see neither and this is the only hint of hope I've felt in months. I'm scared, Pat. What if this is not His will? What if I'm so far off track He can't even see me? What if I'm so far off track I can't see His will or even hear His voice?"

"Calm down, Mel. Take a deep breath. You know God sees you. If this is His will, and I believe it is, He will work it out. Now's the time to stand on your faith and trust Him, He will not lead you astray. Promise you won't worry this to death and block what He is trying to show you or the blessing He wants to give you."

Melena sighed as peace flowed over her at the confidence in her friend's voice. "You're right. I promise."

They talked a few more minutes then rang off.

* * * * *

I'm dying. I can't breathe. My heart is going to explode—disintegrate into a million tiny pieces. Will the pain ever ease up? Everyone says it'll get better, that time heals all wounds. Yeah, right. That's all unadulterated bullshit.

Melena's hands curled into fists so tight she nearly snapped the pen in two. She lifted her eyes heavenward and screamed into the empty room.

"I can't do this. Oh, God, why? How am I supposed to do this? Please, Jesus, just take me home..."

Silence. No lightning bolt, no thunder, not even a still, small voice to comfort. The pen bounced off the wall. Her journal followed.

"All right then, enough already! I'm tired of winding up on this rug by my bed. If You're not going to take me home, then please...give me a reason to live."

She pulled herself onto the bed and buried her face in Jon's pillow, yet his scent eluded her. She struggled to her feet, moved to the closet, then his dresser, rifled through his clothing, and came up with nothing. She crumbled, his favorite flannel shirt clasped to her breast. Sobs tore through her in painful torrents.

Spent, she dug in the bedside table drawer for another pen, then picked up her journal once more—

It's been six months today and I still have no meaning or purpose in my life. I don't know why but the three-month marks seem to hit me the hardest. Last month passed by with its share of agony, but today I'm not sure if I can keep going.

When I pray, all I get is: Your life is about to change drastically.

Yeah, like it hasn't already?

I don't know what God is trying to show or tell me! All I know is I've got to make it through this day. There's no one I can talk to. Pat's gone. The kids are wrapped up in their own grief. Mom and Dad are hurting. Jon's mother and father have been long gone and neither his brother nor sister has called or come by in months. It's like I've fallen off the face of their planet. Friends listen, but don't really understand. No one understands.

It would be so easy to end this pain....

Again, the thought entices and yet, I know that is not a solution. What is the answer? To whom can I turn?

Only the Lord.

God, help me hang on.

* * * * *

Melena stared at the computer screen. Fear and excitement

clogged her throat. There it was...the email she'd been waiting for. She nearly fell out of her chair when the doorbell shrilled.

"I'm coming," she hollered, then pushed back from the desk and hurried to see who would be so bold as to visit this late. Peeking through the curtain, she was relieved to see Pat standing on her step. She opened the door. Pat enfolded her in a hug then stepped inside.

"Well, have you heard anything yet?"

Melena turned, speaking over her shoulder as she walked toward the kitchen. "The email is sitting in my inbox. The subject line gives no indication of the answer. I've stared at it for hours, my emotions on a rollercoaster." She held out her hands. "Look, I'm a wreck, afraid to open it, afraid not to."

She fiddled with the coffee pot, dropped the filter and spilled grounds until with a snort, Pat pushed her out of the way and did the deed herself.

"For the past couple of weeks, I've gone back and forth with God, torn between excitement and hope—knowing I'll receive the grant, and fear and dread that I won't." Melena sat at the table, and then hopped up to pace. "I've researched the distance to drive, twelve hours, compared to cost and time of flying then renting a car and driving from San Antonio to Utopia.

"I've told my family about the Crossed Penn Ranch and the artists retreat. They all agree it would be neat if I won. I've done the math with my finances over and over and, should I not receive the grant, I could afford a weekend at the Crossed Penn, maybe a week, at the most. But then what? Dare I spend that money, especially with nothing going back into my savings? I'm such a mess!"

Pat grabbed her by the shoulders and gave a slight shake then took Melena's hand and all but dragged her into the office. "Just open the email already!"

Melena sent up a silent plea, placed the cursor over the email and huffed a sigh. "Okay...here goes nothing..."

She closed her eyes while Pat read the email aloud then lunged from her chair and tugged Pat into her arms. "I won! I'm going to Utopia, Texas! Thank You, Jesus!"

Pat pulled her into an impromptu dance around the office. "Congratulations! I knew you'd get it!"

Dizzy with excitement, Melena dropped into the chair. "Oh, my goodness, now what? Should I drive or fly?"

"I'd say drive. It's bound to be a lovely trip. Leave a couple of days early and take in the sights and sounds. Explore. Make it an adventure."

Melena shook her head. "I can't do this!"

"Yes, you can!"

"What will I wear? I only own one pair of jeans."

Pat rolled her eyes. "So, we'll go shopping."

Melena massaged her throbbing temples, the excitement replaced by concern. "Have you priced jeans lately?"

Pat grinned at the frustrated disappointment in her friend's tone. "Same old Melena, so conscientious. I swear, you put more consideration into a grocery list than most people would an entire month of shopping," she said with a chuckle. "I absolutely love that about you, but have you ever thought of shopping at second-hand stores and thrift shops?"

Melena gasped. Her skin chilled then heated. "Jon would never have allowed that."

Pat chuckled. "Nor would you have deigned to question or second-guess him. But, Mel, there are some pretty upscale second-hand shops with really nice clothes."

"I don't know if I can do this, Pat. I've never ventured out on my own. I've never been away from home, alone, for two weeks."

Pat knelt at her feet, her expression gentle, her gaze determined. "About time, if you ask me."

Melena frowned. "What do you mean?"

Pat chewed on her lip. Tension rose between them until she took Melena's hands in hers and kissed the back of each. "Mel, you're my best friend and you know I love you more than words can express. I loved Jon too and the kids are like my own, but it's time you stop concerning yourself with everyone's needs and wants. Stop weighing and measuring every decision to death, and for once, think about what *you* want. What *you* need.

"You've given your life in service to others...parents, husband, children, church, community, even your job...and there's nothing wrong with that. But God has something more for you in this life. He's trying to show you something here—trying to get you to dream a new dream, to show you a new plan, a new purpose for your life. Or maybe His original plan and purpose. We all have a destiny He has designed for us.

"Now, I'm not saying Jon wasn't part of His destiny for you, but he was *your* choice. *Your* dream was to be married and have a family and God honored that. Anyone can look around and see He did.

But…" She hesitated.

Melena remained silent, absorbing every word.

"But I believe God has more for you than being a wife and mother. A greater vision than you've ever thought or imagined. His word even says so. Heck, I don't know, Mel—and this might make no sense to you right now, but I believe there is a *reason* why Jon went home to be with the Lord and you're still here." She rose to her feet, pulling Melena with her and into a hug. "Open your mind and your spirit. Broaden your horizons and enlarge your vision. What brings you happiness? Think outside the boxes you've put yourself in."

Melena clung to her friend a moment then stepped back with a sigh. "It's so overwhelming, Pat. I don't know how else to explain these emotions, these thoughts and fears. I've never been so indecisive in my life. So unsettled. I mean for the past thirty years I've known the exact who, what, when, where and why of every detail of my life. Now I have no idea and it scares the daylights out of me."

Pat closed her eyes and inhaled, then exhaled on a sigh. "I can only imagine, but you've been given a gift here, Mel, an opportunity you never would have sought on your own while Jon was alive. Promise you'll take advantage of God's goodness and not talk yourself out of it."

Melena's lips quirked. "I wish you could go with me. You're so much stronger than I am, so much more adventurous."

Humor danced in Pat's gaze. She shrugged. "Who knows, I just might find a way up to the Texas Hill Country at some point while you're there."

Melena laughed. "Guess I need a cell phone now. The kids will be happy. They've been trying to drag me into the twenty-first century for years. They were ecstatic when I bought my laptop."

Pat shook her head. "No, you don't have to get a cell phone. Have your vehicle hooked up with that new-fangled satellite service that tracks your whereabouts if there's an emergency and get a phone card if you have to, in order to call home. But limit your calls. You can give the ranch's phone numbers to the family in case of an emergency but take these two weeks to yourself without being so accessible to others or having them easily accessible to you."

Melena's eyes widened. "You really think I can go two whole weeks without contact with my family?"

Pat shrugged. "I don't know if you can, but I do know it wouldn't hurt to try. Think of this time as a spiritual retreat or something where it's just you and God. Someplace far away with no cell phone service, no internet or fax machines. You can always call me, anytime, day or night and I'll keep you posted. I'll be here anyway and don't mind being your proxy with the family. Or better yet, don't call. Just close your eyes and think of me and I'll be there in spirit. Have a doubt or fear? Think of what I would say or do and do it. Whatever, just take some time and listen to your soul. Listen to your spirit."

She hugged Melena again. "I've got to go now, and you need to get some rest. Let me know when you make your arrangements and I'll help you get things sorted out and packed."

They walked to the door. Pat leaned in and gave her a kiss on the cheek.

"Congratulations again! It'll be fun—and don't let any thought except how much fun it'll be enter your mind."

Melena promised, then locked up after her friend walked out the door. Later she sat in her bed, journal in hand.

Can I do this?

Pat seems so sure. I wish I had her confidence.

She closed her eyes and let her friend's exuberance flow through her entire being. "I will *not* let fear steal the joy of this moment," she determined aloud, then wrote the declaration in all caps and put the pen away.

"I'll figure out the details tomorrow. Tonight I'm going to just be happy I was awarded the grant and relish the feel of having a reason to be happy." She hugged the journal to her breast and turned out the light.

The next morning, she awoke with a smile on her face and a sense of excitement and hope she hadn't experienced since Jon's illness. She spent the next two hours on the phone with her parents and children. Everyone was ecstatic and supportive. She turned on her stereo, put several CD's into the multi-disc deck and spent the better part of the morning dancing and singing along with the praise music.

Exhausted and exhilarated at the same time, she took a walk, then returned home, pulled her painting supplies out of the closet and set to work. Inspiration drove her deep into the night until her eyes blurred and fingers cramped. She pushed away from the easel, dropped brushes in turpentine, closed the paint caddy and, for the first time in months, fell into a dreamless slumber.

* * * * *

Seven months ago today I buried the love of my life. I have no idea how I've made it this far through the valley of the shadow of death.

For that is what grief is. Many nights I long to lie down in this world and wake up with Jon in the next. Mornings are still difficult. We used to sit and talk over coffee. Now I sit alone.

And my heart weeps.

I move from room to room, never staying in one spot, but it makes no difference. The emptiness is acute—like a sharp knife to the soul. The silence is deafening. Except for a lone cry in the dark like the eerie moan of a wayward wind.

It hurts.

Everything about this place I'm in, hurts—physically, mentally, emotionally, spiritually. Will I ever be free of the pain? I finally realized why Jon keeps appearing so alive in my dreams—because he is alive with Christ.

Words rise in my spirit...God will heal your grief if you release it.

I'd love to know how to do this.

God will use this pain to help others if you let Him.

How can I help others with their grief when mine is still so raw, so deep?

There's a purpose for your life, a reason Jon could no longer be a part of it.

What, God? Whatever is it You would have me do that he couldn't be at my side? It makes no sense! Nothing makes a bit of sense anymore. I'll be so glad when I'm on the road to Utopia. Maybe once ensconced in the Texas Hill Country I'll find meaning and purpose in all of this.

Chapter Four

The next few days passed in a flurry of activity. Melena packed and repacked her suitcase at least a dozen times before settling on a couple pair of jeans, capris, shorts, and lots of T-shirts and tank tops. She bought a pair of boots at a thrift store, had her car serviced and the new-fangled satellite service installed.

She stopped by the cemetery on her way out of town, knelt on Jon's grave, and talked with him. "Well, I'm on my way. I decided to drive to the Crossed Penn Ranch. The twelve-hour trip shouldn't be too hard, but I'm taking Pat's advice and splitting it up. I'll spend the night somewhere in Louisiana about halfway there. I hurt at the thought of leaving for two weeks, and yet I know I need this. God wouldn't have worked it out if He didn't want me to be there. We'll see..."

She swiped the moisture off her cheeks, pressed trembling fingers to her lips then traced the name carved in granite. "I love you," she whispered then stood and walked away. Her decision wavered with every step, but she determined not to look back, turn around, or change her mind.

She was going on this retreat.

She didn't stop crying until she crossed the state line.

* * * * *

Melena pulled in at the rest area and visitors' bureau just inside the Louisiana border with a sigh of relief. She unbuckled the seatbelt, grabbed her purse and climbed out of the car with a groan. Four hours into the trip and she was stiff and sore, and her bladder threatened to burst at any moment. After relieving herself of the numerous cups of coffee she'd drank along the way, she decided to walk around a bit, glad she had taken Pat's advice and left a day early in order to enjoy the drive. She retrieved her camera and walked down to the pond a few hundred yards away from the building. After a dozen or so pictures, she wandered into the visitors' center where a perky teenager behind the service counter greeted her.

"Hi!"

Melena smiled. "Hello, yourself."

"Beautiful day. Are you traveling for business or pleasure?"

"Well, not sure how you'd categorize my trip, to be honest. I'm on my way to an artists' retreat in Utopia, Texas. I'm sure there'll be lots of both once I get there, though."

The youngster's eyes widened. "You're an artist? I love to draw! What's your name? Have I heard of you? What kind of art do you do?"

Melena held up a hand with a tiny laugh. "Hold on. One question at a time please."

The girl turned several shades of red. "Sorry."

Melena put her purse on the counter and leaned in to pat her on the shoulder. She peered at the name tag attached to the girl's blouse. "No problem...Missy. My name is Melena Rhyker, and no, you probably haven't heard of me. I've never thought of myself as an artist. Until recently, I've only painted for pleasure or created something as a gift for someone. What do you like to draw?"

"Anything! I mean, sometimes I just wake up in the middle of the night with these ideas and can only rest once I've sketched them out."

"Ah, the sign of a true artist. Do you keep a sketch pad with you always?"

Missy flushed and nodded. "All the time. My boyfriend swears it's an extension of me."

Melena laughed. "Well, don't ever stop. Art is a wonderful gift, a talent given to you from God and it pleases Him when you use it."

Again, the girl flushed. "Thank you. I always wondered about that."

The phone rang. Missy answered it and put the caller on hold, then smiled at Melena once more. "I'm glad you stopped in. I hope you have fun on your retreat. You should blog about it so others can experience it with you."

"Blog?"

Missy nodded. "Yeah, you know, an online journal or web log. A blog."

Melena frowned. "I've been a bookkeeper and administrative assistant all of my life. I've heard of those but never had a use for one. Nor had I ever thought I'd need one. What purpose would it serve?"

"Hang on, let me catch this call and I'll explain it to you. If you're not in a hurry, that is."

Melena shook her head then walked around the room and examined the various brochures and artwork depicting Louisiana wildlife, festivals and culture while she waited for Missy to finish her call. Before she could turn back to the counter, the phone rang again, twice, and a couple of visitors wandered in asking for directions to some town a few miles away.

Missy bid them goodbye with a warm laugh then waved Melena over. "It never fails, just when I find someone I can really talk to, I get swamped."

Melena chuckled.

Missy pulled a laptop out from under the counter, hit a few keys and turned it to face Melena. "This is my blog."

Melena read a few entries and looked at the sample sketches the girl had scanned and uploaded to the site. "Wow. You're very good."

Missy beamed. "It's kind of like an online diary. For me anyway. People use blogs for all sorts of things. You should get one. I'll subscribe if you do and follow your retreat and tell my friends too. You can upload photos, sketches, or actual paintings if you can scan or photograph them and you can write about your experiences. It'll be great!"

"How do I get one of these things? I mean, I have a website. That was a royal pain in the butt to create. I have no idea how to do a blog."

"What's your website address?"

Melena told her and watched as Missy pulled up her site.

"Who did your site for you?"

The teenager's frown and tone of voice caused heat to flame Melena's cheeks. "I did."

Missy's expression softened. "I'm sorry...I didn't mean to sound negative. It's not a bad site."

"But?"

"Well, you need to showcase your work better. This is some of your work, right?"

Melena nodded.

"It's really great!" Missy said. "But in the world of art, presentation is everything."

"What would you do differently?"

Two hours later Melena left the visitors bureau with a newly revised, more colorful, picturesque website, as well as a blog set up in conjunction with her site. Her mind swarmed with ideas on marketing, making the most of her online presence, and ways to interact with other artists and bring recognition to her work. Thankfully, Missy had written everything down, otherwise she'd never remember it all. She also had the girl's email address and a promise to exchange correspondence often and to stop back by on her return home.

A hundred and fifty miles farther down the road, she pulled into a truck stop, topped off her gas tank and entered the restaurant to fill her empty stomach. She found the payphone, pulled the card of pre-paid minutes out of her purse and dialed her son's number to check in with him. She'd promised to touch base with at least one family member or Pat who, in turn, would relay the specifics of their conversation to the others. After the call and a hot meal, she grabbed a bag of snacks and drinks from the convenience store, then drove to the nearest hotel and checked into a room for the night.

She unloaded her suitcase and briefcase, did some stretches to work the kinks out of her body then took a long, hot shower and curled up in bed with her laptop. After logging in to her new blog, Melena was surprised to find several people had already subscribed to follow her posts. She recapped her adventures of the day, uploaded a few photos she'd taken along the way and thanked her new friend Missy for all of her help. She shut down the computer and pulled her journal out of the bag to record her more personal thoughts and feelings. A blog might be fine, good and well to share her professional life, but her deepest feelings were for God alone.

She awoke the next morning surprised to find sunlight streaming through the curtains. One glance at the clock had her jolting upright. Nine o'clock? She hadn't slept this late in years, or so well in months. Throwing back the covers, she padded to the counter and fumbled with the small coffee pot, wishing she'd thought to prepare it the night before. The machine hissed and spit then happily gurgled the aromatic brew into the carafe.

Melena splashed water on her face and stared at herself in the mirror for long moments. As shocked as she'd been to sleep so late, she was even more surprised to see no dark circles or furrows of grief reflected in the face looking back at her. She leaned closer. "You're going to make it," she promised. "By the grace of God, you're going to get through this valley of death and into new life. Whatever that might entail."

Moisture welled up in her eyes, rolled down her cheeks and she wished she'd just kept her mouth shut. "Should have just thanked God for the good night's rest and left well enough alone."

She buried her face in a towel and cried.

An hour later, she was on her way. The trip through Louisiana passed without a hitch. Lots of green, lots of water and though pretty, nothing that astounded or made her want to stop and explore. The first few hours in Texas were no different.

Until she turned off the interstate, headed north, and ventured into the Hill Country.

She stopped more than once to soak in the beauty of rock and sky, took dozens of photographs, and arrived at the Crossed Penn as the sun set. Although she'd called earlier to inform the staff she would be checking in late, she apologized for any inconvenience and was met with no reproof, only open acceptance by the owners themselves. Once settled in her room, she sought out the guest phone downstairs. She had spoken to her mother earlier and promised to call her daughter the next day, so this call was to Pat.

"I made it, and oh my gosh, Pat, this place is gorgeous! This Hill Country must be the best kept secret Texas has!"

Pat laughed. "Aren't you glad you listened to me and took your time driving up?"

"Oh, yes. I've got dozens of photos to put on my blog now! And guess what? I passed through Bandera—the 'cowboy capital of the world.'"

"Really? Now *that* sounds like the place to visit."

Knowing Pat's penchant for cowboys, Melena laughed. "Yeah, it does look like a great place to visit. I have to pass back through on my way home, so might just have to stay a day or so."

"Oh, no, you don't, girlfriend! You wait until we can go back together. So tell me about this place you're at."

"The Crossed Penn is everything their website and brochures promised. The lodge is enormous and there are individual cabins all around. My room is on the second floor of the main house. They have a swimming pool and a fitness center, with whirlpools and saunas for men and women."

"You mean separate saunas and whirlpools for men and women? It's the twenty-first century for crying out loud."

Melena laughed. "Yeah, but not everyone is as liberal as you think.

But don't worry, there's a coed one also for those who are. They offer horseback riding, hiking and fossil digging. Of course, there are art classes and large blocks of time scheduled for artistry, but when not studying or working, we're pretty much on our own. From what I can understand there are a variety of artists here who do any number of things—from pencil art to sculpting and everything in between and I'm looking forward to meeting them. It's so wonderful, Pat, and from just one meeting, I can tell you, these people are amazing!

"The ranch owners, Anne & Bill Penn are artists in their own right. He sculpts and paints. She does photography. You should see some of the stuff displayed throughout the lodge. Together they've carved out a niche perfect for nurturing the spirit, especially a creative one. The staff is extremely personable and easy to talk with. The cowboys tip their hats and call me 'ma'am'."

She giggled. "It all seems so quaint and slightly unreal—like I'm walking onto a movie set or something."

"That's great, Mel. Really great. I'm so glad you didn't talk yourself out of this. I'll pass the word on to the family that you're safe and sound at the ranch. Now I know you promised to check in often, but don't do so out of obligation. You can always email and, believe it or not, the kids and your parents have subscribed to your blog. We'll know how you are doing by what you post, so don't feel like you *have* to call. Give yourself time to be alone and listen to your spirit."

Melena sighed. "I will," she promised then rang off and returned to her room.

* * * * *

Two days later, Melena updated her blog—

Purple sunsets, sunrises layered in various shades of gold—I've heard these expressions, seen breathtaking artwork depicting them but never thought I'd witness such beauty as the sun rising or setting the way it does in Texas Hill Country. Oh, I've seen the mountains in Colorado and Montana while vacationing with the family and thought them majestic, but there's just something special about these hills...a coziness and a serenity I haven't felt before. Almost like I've come home. Crazy, I know. I have a home and a life in Mississippi.

She uploaded photos and since her family and friends were following her posts, she knew they'd want to know how she was doing emotionally, so she added an assurance just for them...

I've made it an entire day without crying.

There's peace in these hills.

Chapter Five

Melena jumped, startled when someone pounded on her door. "Who is it?"

"Hollie."

Melena scrambled to let her in.

"Get dressed. We're all going dancing."

Her eyes widened. "I haven't been dancing in so long, I doubt I remember how."

"Like riding a bicycle," Hollie assured.

Melena glanced at the clock. "But it's nearly nine o'clock!"

Hollie shook her head. "Band doesn't start until nine anyway. C'mon, it'll do you good. It'll do us all good...the sights, sounds, experience. Think of it as research."

Melena laughed and threw all caution to the wind. Fifteen minutes later, she met the gang of artists and ranch hands in the lodge room. They all piled into a couple of vans and took off to the most popular honky-tonk around. Some of them took to the dance floor right off, others waited until they'd had enough alcohol to loosen their inhibitions. Melena fell in-between. A couple of two-steps, a waltz, and several line-dances after they arrived, she sat at the table sipping a wine spritzer. Billy, otherwise known as *Kidd* because of his age and reported ancestry, approached.

"Why so pensive?"

Everyone knew her marital status. Still Melena hesitated in sharing her thoughts, much less grief, with a stranger. She smiled and shrugged. "It's just been a long time since I've been out like this."

Billy pulled up a chair. "Mind if I sit?"

"Of course not."

"I know this is a tough time for you. Been there myself. But it's okay to enjoy the evening."

Melena's eyes widened at his statement and the sympathy reflected in his gentle gaze. Her eyebrow arched in question. Billy nodded.

"Lost my wife when we were twenty. Only married a few years compared to you, but it still sucked."

Her lips trembled at the admission. "I'm so sorry. I wouldn't wish this kind of pain on my worst enemy."

"Neither would I. Happened a long time ago, but I still remember the agony. If you ever want a shoulder or an ear, I'll do my best."

She smiled. "Thank you."

Billy upended his beer and took a deep pull on the longneck. "Now, how about that dance?"

Before she could protest, he had her out on the floor.

* * * * *

The next morning Melena sat, journal in hand.

A couple of the cowboys took a few of us dancing last night. I'd forgotten how much I love to do that! Jon and I used to go all the time— until life, work, and raising kids took up all of our time and energy. Dancing the night away was another thing we looked forward to doing again. Will there ever come a time when not every thought revolves around what we used to do and looked forward to? Will there ever be a day when I can think of my life without him in it? Will this be another milestone by which I measure my life—before Jon, after Jon?

I look back over the last week and realize I've cried less, smiled and laughed more since I arrived here. There is definitely something special about this place, these people. My artwork has improved. The piece I'm working on is currently done in watercolors, but will be painted on canvas. I can even envision it on glass, which excites me, gives me hope, and makes me believe quitting my job was a good decision. Still have no idea what I'll do when the money runs out. Can't think that far ahead, too overwhelming.

"One day at a time," the Lord says.

God help me trust that You are working all things together for my good even though I don't understand, and to trust You one day at a time.

She put the journal away and climbed out of bed. Every muscle protested as she made her way into the bathroom. Donning her swimsuit and matching wrap, she slipped her feet into sandals, grabbed a towel and joined several others, Hollie included, in the women's whirlpool.

"How is everyone this morning?"

Hollie's groan could be heard above the others. "Tired, sore, and hung over."

Melena laughed. "I feel wonderful! A bit sore, I'll admit, but other than that, I'm great. Thank you for inviting me. I'd forgotten how much fun a night out dancing could be."

Sarah, another artist in residence glared at her through one eye. "How come you're not hung over? I saw you drinking."

Melena smirked. "A little secret I learned a long time ago. Not that we've ever been big drinkers. Just an occasional bottle of wine, a couple of drinks with dinner, or a night cap in front of the fireplace."

"Pray tell," Sarah breathed.

"Stick with the same drink, don't over-indulge, alternate with water instead of soft drinks, and no shots... jello, tequila or otherwise."

Hollie moaned, then smiled. "Remind us next time, will you?"

Melena chuckled and promised, then settled in as the others climbed out one by one and headed elsewhere. The gentle hum of water jets and bubbles were like a lullaby in the quiet room and she allowed her thoughts to drift until only peace remained. Thirty minutes later, she rose, tied the towel around her and slipped into the sauna, glad to find it empty. Stretching out on a bench, she adjusted her swimsuit and once more allowed her mind, body and spirit to relax.

With the energy of a wet noodle, she eased out of the sauna, rinsed the sweat off her skin, and tied the sarong around her waist. She tossed the damp towel over her shoulders, put on her sandals and headed to her room to shower and change. Fresh fruit and pastries left over from breakfast lay spread out at the buffet like a feast for the famished. Melena filled a plate and had taken two steps toward the stairs when Anne Penn entered the room flanked by a handsome hunk of man Melena hadn't seen before.

"Hi, Melena. I'd like you to meet Garrett, our new part-time wrangler, part-time maintenance man."

Eyes the color of Texas bluebonnets swept over her in a gaze as potent as a caress, then locked with hers. A dimple danced in the cowboy's cheek when he tipped his hat and grinned.

"Ma'am," he drawled.

Melena tugged the ends of her towel together and down over her skimpily clad bosom, muttered a quick hello, and escaped. Racing up the stairs as fast as possible on legs that wobbled, she entered her room, all but dropped the plate on her nightstand, and sat down onto the bed.

Never had she felt the pure sexual punch of such raw masculinity in a single look.

Goosebumps rose on her flesh. Beads of sweat popped across her brow. Melena shivered, wiped them off with the towel then buried her face in hands that shook. She tried to will some semblance of order to her scrambling pulse and untangle the mass of nerves in her stomach.

Moments later, she stood and walked into the bathroom. One glance in the mirror and she groaned. *How mortifying!* Though her skin boasted a nice, rosy glow, her shoulder-length hair was a snarled mess of riotous black curls. She closed her eyes as embarrassment washed over her in angry waves. "Great first impression, Lord," she muttered, then sighed. "Oh, well, nothing a little anti-frizz serum and a flat iron can't cure."

A half hour later, clean and fully clothed, Melena tamed her coarse, unruly locks into a sleek, layered style. By the time she finished and unplugged her hair utensils, she'd convinced herself everything she experienced in her encounter with Garrett-the-new-wrangler-maintenance-whatever guy was nothing more than the combination of ambiance and atmospheric conditions brought on by her time in the sauna and whirlpool.

The lunch bell rang. Melena chose to bypass the crowd and took her slightly wilted fruit into the studio.

"Coward," a little voice whispered.

Maybe so. She pressed a hand to her midriff to quell an entire kaleidoscope of butterflies doing the jitterbug in her stomach. *But I can't handle seeing him again just yet.*

Enclosed, with only the sights and smells of the studio, Melena relaxed. She sat on the stool behind her easel, closed her eyes and let the excitement of last night fill her senses. Like a slide show, images crowded her mind and exploded onto paper in bursts of color. Soft pastels around the bar, bold strokes on the dance floor, vibrant, energetic shades around the band. She painted until her mind blurred and fingers cramped, then sat back to examine the work with a keen eye. *Oh yeah.* Every detail was etched in perfection and she itched to see it in glass.

Melena rose from the stool only to slump back down when a wave of weakness washed over her. A glance at her watch confirmed she'd worked for two solid hours. Her stomach grumbled, reminding her she'd only eaten a sparse plate of fruit. After last night's activities and her time in the whirlpool and sauna this morning, she needed more sustenance if she expected to work efficiently. She eased off the stool and put her supplies away then washed up and went downstairs, hoping to ferret out something to hold her over until dinner.

The ache behind her eyes and the knots in her neck and shoulders convinced her that the glass art could wait until tomorrow, so she headed upstairs to her room. Sarah and Hollie were caught up in an animated discussion as Melena passed by the sitting area on the second floor. They noticed her before she could slip by and waved her in.

"OMG, did you see the new wrangler?" Sarah asked.

Melena avoided direct eye contact, but her cheeks grew warm with the memory of that one meeting. "I met him this morning."

"Isn't he the most incredible man?" Hollie hummed. "I mean...wow!"

Melena shrugged. "He's nice looking."

"Nice looking?" A perfect unison response—tones incredulous, eyes wide.

"The man is a virtual feast for sore eyes," Hollie asserted. "This guy is the epitome of cowboy with a capital C...wide shoulders, broad chest, narrow waist, slim hips, long, muscular legs and the way those jeans fit...oh *my*."

"Yeah, like heroes of the old West, the stuff love stories are made of," Sarah added.

Jon's voice rose in her mind, teasing about the cowboy romances she used to read. She sucked in a deep breath to quell her emotions. "Ladies, please. It's not polite to talk about the man like this. After all, he is flesh and blood, a human being with thoughts and feelings. Not an object to be drooled over."

"Yeah, but there's nothing wrong with a little appreciation for so much eye candy." Sarah heaved a lusty sigh.

Melena shook her head and excused herself from the conversation, but once alone in her room her thoughts spiraled out of control. She picked up her journal and pen and rushed to keep up with them—

Eye candy. Yeah, but he's more than that. His smile lights up the entire room. And those eyes...

He tipped his hat and called me "Ma'am," then our gazes met and I felt some kind of connection. My heart kicked a little, spirit leapt. Weird, I know, but I'm at a loss for words on how to explain...

Is it wrong for me to feel this way, or to look at a man with appreciation after only seven months of widowhood?

"Oh, God..."

Hello, guilt.

"Another emotion to add to my insanity."

I hear Jon's voice, "Our vows are till death do us part, Mel, not death and a year. Not even death and a day."

We talked about this often in our years of marriage and he always said if he died before me, he wanted me to go on living, to not give up, to be happy, and to love again. Of course, I said the same thing to him...but how is that even possible when all I want is my husband back? I never pictured my life without him. I still can't. When I try to think of the future, I either see Jon or a big, black...?...and then the questions start...Why? How? What now?

So many questions and with them so much pain. Will I ever understand? Will I ever heal or be whole?

"To hell with all that, just a little peace would be nice. I've found that here and I'm not about to let some handsome cowboy and a couple of hormonal, eccentric girls shatter it!"

Firm in her resolve, she put away the journal and pen, stretched out on her bed and dozed.

She dreamed of Jon.

And wept.

* * * * *

Melena grabbed her camera, slipped out of her room and tiptoed down the stairs, anxious to get away from the other retreat attendees. Their time here was winding down and so far, she'd done very little exploring on her own. But today, this morning at least, she wanted nothing more than to be alone. The soft squeak of her shoes across the stone floor marred the quiet as she exited through the lodge room, not wanting the cowbell on the other door to disturb anyone. The huge rocking chairs on the porch beckoned. She couldn't resist. Plopping down in one, she watched the sun begin its rise over the hills, brightening the morning in various degrees of light and color.

A movement by the pool drew her attention. Melena leaned forward in her chair to get a better view of who or what was down there and watched as Garrett pulled himself out of the water and proceeded to do pushups on the concrete ledge. *Oh my*. Sensations, raw and unfamiliar, whispered across her skin. He glanced up, waved. Grinned.

Tiny bubbles of heat burst in her cheeks. Melena lunged from the chair and walked in the opposite direction. Before long she got so engrossed in taking pictures of the scenery around her, the incident slid from her mind. Until breakfast. When she saw him at the serving table next to Bob, wearing an apron, she put the camera between them and snapped pictures. He chuckled.

"I hope you don't plan to post those anywhere."

"Not sure yet what I'll do with them, but whatever setting I use, the title will be 'working cowboy.'"

"Then you should wait and take pictures at Cowboy Breakfast down by the arena. They'll be more authentic then."

"There's a thought." She reached for a plate. Their hands touched. After a quick, electrified moment, he moved away and allowed her to get her food before preparing his own tray. Melena excused herself and carried her meal up to her room where she choked down a few precious bites before the activities planned for that day began.

* * * * *

The days flew by on the wings of time, each one a new adventure filled with art classes and instruction. Trail rides and group hikes led by Garrett or Kidd comingled with hours alone in the studio or her room. Before she knew it, her two-week stay was up.

Melena tossed things carelessly into the suitcase and overnight bag. "It's open," she barked when someone knocked on the door.

Sarah walked in. "Hey, Melena, I brought you my business card. We promised to stay in touch."

Melena slammed the suitcase shut and jerked the zipper closed with hands that shook.

"Just put it on the nightstand. Mine are there, take one." Her voice sounded harsh even to her own ears.

Sarah's voice softened. "Are you okay?"

Melena's lip trembled. "I don't want to go home. There's nothing to go back to. My entire being is screaming in agony. My spirit feels as though it will just wither up and die if I have to return to that house where so much love existed. Once upon a time. But no more. Now there's only pain and emptiness and shattered dreams."

"I'm so sorry," Sarah whispered and opened her arms.

Melena slumped into her new friend's embrace. "Oh, God, why? I don't understand why."

Kidd, who'd offered to carry luggage for the ladies, stepped through the entrance and closed the door behind him. He took Melena's bags off the bed then pulled the women down to sit beside him. Melena on one side, Sarah on the other, he cuddled them both, whispering words of comfort and condolence.

Sarah reached across and stroked Melena's hair off her flushed cheeks. "You know he's in a better place."

"I know that! My head knows, my spirit knows, but I just can't wrap my heart around the fact that he's gone and he's not coming back! Never again will I see him or touch him or hold him in my arms." She gazed up at Kidd. "Does it ever get easier?"

"In time."

* * * * *

That afternoon, Melena checked into a hotel. The dread that filled her made every mile she'd traveled seem like a hundred. She called her parents and children, took a swim in the guest pool and settled in for the evening. She logged onto her computer and found an email from Missy that her work schedule had been changed and she wouldn't be at the Tourist Bureau anytime during Melena's return trip. Which was fine. She didn't feel like visiting a bright, cheery teenager when her spirit was so heavy, her thoughts so dark. She'd stopped in Louisiana for the night. A senseless waste of money she knew, but the thought of returning to that house, that town where everyone knows her, knew Jon. Where everyone saw her as his wife or widow. Foregoing the blog, she pulled out her journal—

Will I ever be just me?

Who am I?

For so long, I was Jon's wife or so-and-so's mother. Now I'm "Jon's widow."

How far is the journey from wife to widow to individual?

How long?

Chapter Six

Melena groaned when the doorbell rang, its sharp drone reverberating in her skull. She'd been home three days and for three days she'd avoided contact with her family

For three days, she cried.

She ate less, drank more, and smoked—something she hadn't done since her teenage rebellion years. And it showed. Her mirror reflected the ghastly sight of haunted eyes, pale, sunken skin, matted hair.

The bell sounded again.

"Go away," she muttered and covered her head with a pillow. The phone shrilled. "What?" she growled into the receiver.

"Open the door," Pat insisted.

"I just want to be left alone."

"Well, I'm not leaving you alone. You've holed yourself up in this house ever since you got back from the retreat, hardly talked to a soul. Your family is frantic. I just got off the phone with your mother. What in the world happened between you two?"

"Don't want to talk about it."

Pat's frustrated growl sounded over the line seconds before Melena jerked the base out of the wall and threw it and the receiver across the room.

"Leave me *alone!*" she screamed then curled up in a ball. "I just want to go home! Jesus, why won't you take me home?" Sobs tore through her in painful torrents but didn't drown out the continued ring of the doorbell. Moments later, Pat tapped on her window.

"Melena, if you don't open that damn door and let me in, I'll call the police to break it down!" she barked through the pane. A stream of profanity sounded through the glass when Melena didn't budge. Pat banged again. "Melena!"

Melena lunged from the bed. "Oh, all right, already! Let me pee first!" She stumbled into the bathroom, took care of business, then fumbled her way to the front door and let Pat in.

"Good grief almighty, look at you!" Pat stepped through the door. Her nose wrinkled. She grabbed Melena by the arm, gave her a slight shake, dragged her into the living room and all but slung her on the couch. "What are you trying to do, kill yourself?"

"If only it were that easy." Melena fell to her knees. "I—I can't do this, P —Pat. I —I don't want to. It hurts." She crossed her arms over her chest for fear if she didn't hold it in, her heart would simply burst through and lie wide open and bleeding all over the floor. "It hurts so much!"

Pat sat beside her, pulled Melena into her arms, and rocked her as though she were a child. "Oh, honey, it'll get better. I don't know when or how, but it's been nearly eight months, Mel, it's bound to get better. One day you'll wake up and the pain won't be as raw or as deep."

"How can you say that? You have no idea!"

"You're right, I've never lost a spouse, but I have lost loved ones. Thought I'd die when Mom and Dad passed away within hours of each other. And I've seen it while ministering to others. Time has a way of making the burden easier to bear. I thought you were so much better with the retreat. What happened?"

Melena sniffed, got a whiff of her own scent and groaned. "Ugh, I need a shower."

Pat helped her to her feet. "Go ahead. I'll clean up and put a pot of coffee on while you get one."

Twenty minutes later, they sat at the kitchen table. Melena fumbled with a napkin. "I've hurt Mom's feelings. Didn't mean to, but we were talking, and I made the comment that I felt I had no reason to come home. She went off on a tangent, ranting and raving that I'm not grateful for the blessings I still have. Of course, I'm grateful. But nothing feels the same. Everything's changed."

She took a sip and tried to put words to the tumultuous emotions. "*I've* changed. The retreat was wonderful. Showed me there's life out there. And that it's okay to live. For the first time since Jon's illness, I felt almost happy."

Guilt rose to choke her. Melena swallowed the hard knot of emotion in her throat. "I *can't* be happy without him. I don't want to."

Pat leaned over and took her hand. Sympathy and understanding glittered in her gaze. "It's okay to be happy, Mel. It *is* okay to live. Jon would want you to."

Melena sighed. "I know, but there's no life here anymore, Pat. The thought of getting back to normal," she finger-quoted the word for emphasis, "to life as it was, which is impossible without Jon, feels so empty. So useless. So...*senseless*." She paused, sipped again.

"You know, I've prayed to be more sensitive to the Holy Spirit, more open to hearing God's voice, and to see what He's trying to show me. But up until the retreat all I ever heard was, 'your life is about to change drastically.'"

She snorted. "Like it hadn't already. But He was right, Pat. My life has changed drastically. I may not know what I want to do with the rest of it, but I know what I don't want—I don't want to be stuck in this house, in this town. I don't even want to be in Mississippi. I know that might sound crazy, but it's how I feel."

"It's not crazy," Pat replied. "It's honest. Any idea yet what you might want to do or where?"

Melena shrugged. "I've wondered if they ever hire people who visited the Crossed Penn to come back and work? Or maybe if another ranch nearby might need help."

"All it would take is a phone call to find out." Pat picked up the phone and handed it to Melena. "The most they can do is say no."

Excitement shivered through her. Melena rushed to where she'd dropped her purse three days ago and scrounged around in it until she found a business card for the ranch. She walked back to the table and dialed the number listed in bold, black numerals. "Here goes nothing..."

Moments later, she hung up the phone with a smile. "They do hire summer help! Shelley, the office manager, is emailing me an application."

Pat rose, then refilled their coffee cups. "Well, I suggest we get online, print it out and get it back to her ASAP."

Melena stood up, only to sway and sit back down. She pressed a hand to her stomach when it growled. "I'm starved."

Pat chuckled. "Let's go grab a bite to eat somewhere. You need to get out of this house anyway. Then we'll come back, and you can get that application done."

An hour later, they returned. Melena booted up her computer, waited while the Wi-Fi connected and logged into her email account. She gasped, overwhelmed at the number of messages in her inbox with *How are you?* or *Please email or call!* in the subject line.

"Oh my, I feel so bad."

"Don't." Pat's voice was sharp. "Guilt is a useless waste of energy."

"But look at how many there are. I've worried everyone to death."

Pat shook her head. "So answer each person. Not each email. Tell them you're okay and you just needed some time alone upon your return. You have a right to your privacy, a right to your grief, and the right to be left alone should you choose without feeling guilty about it."

Melena hugged her friend and smiled. "You are so good for me." She waded through the emails, answered each person, and then she got to the one she really wanted. She opened the attached application, printed it and filled it out. Much like the grant application, the normal information was easy but when she got to the question that asked why she wanted to work on the ranch she halted.

"What am I supposed to say?"

Pat shrugged. "Tell them the truth."

Melena frowned. "You mean that I'm about to lose my mind and need a place to do it?"

Pat laughed. "Well maybe not that much truth."

Melena closed her eyes and asked for God's guidance then, answered the question. *I think the experience would be wonderful and the atmosphere is perfect for healing mind, body and soul.*

She signed the application, scanned the documents and emailed them back to Shelley.

Pat glanced at her watch and sighed. "Wish I could stay longer, but I need to go. Are you going to be all right or should I call someone?"

Melena took her by the hand and led her out of the office and into the foyer. She paused by the door. "I'll be fine. Going to clean this filthy house and call my family."

"Good." Pat nodded. "But don't let them lay a guilt trip on you. Remember what I said...you have a right to your feelings."

Melena hugged her. Emotion welled in her eyes and clogged her throat. "Thank you."

Every ounce of love they felt for each other flowed through Pat's return hug. "Anytime, that's what friends are for. Keep me posted on the application."

"I will."

* * * * *

Melena fumbled with the phone and dialed Pat's number with shaking fingers.

"Hello?"

"I'm going back to the Crossed Penn! Shelley just called and asked how soon I could be there."

"Oh wow, that's great."

"I'm so excited, Pat. And nervous. How on earth am I going to pull this off? What will the kids say? My parents? Until the retreat, I've never been away from them, or away from home, for any length of time."

"It's not about what they think or what they feel, Mel, it's about what you need. Frankly, I think this is the best thing you can do for yourself. It's not like you're moving across country or for good. Just a couple of months. Like I said before, you've got to stop concerning yourself so much with others' thoughts and feelings and just take care of you!"

Melena sighed and rubbed at the tension creasing her brow. "You're right. I've got to do something, and this is the only door God has opened that I can see. My main purpose in life has been taken from me and now I've got to find out what He has for me next. He wouldn't have paved the way for this if it were not His will. So, if for no other reason than to draw closer to Him, which is so much more possible there than here, I am going to do this. The family can support me or just deal with it."

Pat cheered.

Melena laughed. "Now where do I start? What about the house, the bills? There's so much to consider!"

Pat chortled. "Easy. Make sure there's enough money in your checking account to cover your regular bills for the next couple of months. Set them up on automatic bank draft or online bill pay. Line up your kids and parents to pick up your mail and walk through the house every couple of days. We'll shop the thrift stores for a few pair of jeans. Pack lots of T-shirts, tank tops and capris along with tennis shoes, sandals and boots and you're all set."

* * * * *

Two weeks later Melena sat in her bed for the last night before her trip back to Utopia. Tomorrow she'd be on her way. Funny, a month ago she'd left for the retreat. Who would have guessed she'd be heading back to work? Excitement settled in the pit of her stomach. She picked up the checklist she'd written for being gone so long and read over the notes.

She'd never dreamed there were so many details to take care of. She'd even broken down and bought a cell phone. Her kids were ecstatic. Melena chuckled at the memory of their conversations.

Though initially in an uproar, the family seemed to accept, if not understand, her need to do this, to have time and space to figure out the rest of her life.

As if she could do that in a couple of months.

The hardest part would be leaving Jon. She visited the cemetery every day and honestly felt he supported her in this. Heaven knows she needed to find peace and wholeness. Maybe she'd find both in the Hill Country.

We'll see...

She placed the paper on the nightstand and turned out the light. Sleep, when it came wasn't peaceful but filled with disjointed dreams and visions that made no sense to her waking mind when she opened her eyes the next morning. Fear gripped her insides and she wrestled with a million reasons to call and tell Anne she'd changed her mind. The still, soft voice of her innermost being encouraged her to stick to the plan. She left a little later than she'd wanted to, and turned around more than once, fighting panic and uncertainty. Determination born of despair kept her moving forward.

Two days later she logged onto her computer and updated her blog...

It's 4:15 a.m. and I've been up for an hour. I'm staying in the main lodge until the bunkhouse is ready. Probably a couple of days at most.

Her fingers halted, mind blanked. She'd never shared her deepest or darkest thoughts and emotions online and hesitated now in sharing those moments of madness for all the world to see. Taking a minute to quiet her thoughts, she focused on the best parts of her trip.

Though long, the drive up yesterday was nice. Stretches of silent prayer interspersed with praise music. Even tuned into a country & western station a time or two. Need to get reacquainted with boot stomping music again since that is all they listen to here. Well, there is usually classical on in the studio, but everywhere else is country. Finally snuck downstairs and ferreted out a cup of yesterday's coffee. Better than nothing, I guess. Heated in the microwave, it's actually quite good. As soon as the sun comes up, I'm going to take a walk. It's a mile down to the gate, two round-trip. Walking this terrain is bound to do me more good than the high-school track at home. I'll take a few pictures and post them later or tomorrow.

She closed with her customary blessing, posted the entry, shut down the computer and prepared for the day ahead. Not sure exactly what she would be doing today or if she'd even work, she dressed in jeans, a t-shirt and hiking shoes then grabbed her camera and headed out for a walk just as the sun rose.

Fingers of orange and yellow reached down to bathe the rocks in rich shades of peach and cream as the gray of dawn gave way to the hope of morning. Melena paused often to snap photos of the gorgeous sunrise and the wildlife out and about. She saw a jackrabbit and a roadrunner. Stopping, she closed her eyes, took a deep breath, and lifted her face toward the sun. Peace and awe filled her soul.

"Oh, God, it is so beautiful here, so peaceful. Thank You for opening the door for me to come back. I know You're going to use this place to help me, but Lord, use me in this place."

A vehicle approached. Melena stepped off the road to let it pass, surprised when it stopped instead. The window rolled down and the chef, Bob, whom she'd met while attending the retreat, greeted her.

"Nice morning, isn't it?"

Melena nodded. "It sure is."

"Heard you was coming back to work a while. I'm sure you'll be helping in the kitchen on occasion."

"Not sure what I'll be doing as far as work yet. Doesn't really matter though—it's not about the job, it's about the experience."

He chuckled. "I'll remind you of that in a couple of weeks. Guests can be bothersome sometimes. Especially the artistic types."

Melena grinned. "I hope we weren't too bothersome while I was here for the retreat."

A hint of crimson darkened his cheeks, but Bob had the grace to laugh. "Not that I can recall. Better get on down there now and start breakfast. You eating?"

Melena nodded. "Yes, and I'd give my right arm for a fresh cup of coffee."

Bob chuckled. "A lovely arm it is, but not necessary. Finish your walk and it'll be ready when you get back up to the lodge." He put his truck in gear and rolled away.

Melena walked a bit farther, took a couple more photos, and then returned to the lodge. After putting the camera away in her room, she went down to the kitchen and offered to help.

Bob shook his head and handed her a cup. "Time enough for that once you're officially on the payroll. You just relax and enjoy your day."

Melena thanked him, took her cup and went out on the porch to sit in one of the rocking chairs. She sipped coffee and enjoyed the stillness. Unlike the acute, empty silence at home, this seemed more like an expectant pause, a moment pregnant with promise. And for the brief span of time, she relished the quiet.

After breakfast, Shelley handed her an employee packet. "After I'm done with the guests checking in and out, we'll talk."

Melena took the packet into the dining room, poured a fresh cup of coffee, filled out the required forms and read the handbook. She'd finished and poured another cup when Shelley called her into the office.

"I can't express my gratitude enough for you giving me the chance to come back here." Melena rushed into a thank-you speech.

"I'll remind you of that often, I'm sure," Shelley replied with a laugh. "Many people come for the summer thinking it'll be like a working vacation but believe me, it can get hectic. Especially when we're booked."

"That's okay. I really need something different right now and I believe God opened this door just for me."

Shelley nodded. "Okay, well the new pay period starts on Monday, so for the next couple of days you can just settle in and relax. I'll have you shadow Marcey in housekeeping tomorrow. She'll show you how to clean rooms and do the laundry. Today you can piddle in the kitchen with Bob if you want and maybe visit with Kidd in the corral. We'll have the bunkhouse ready for you to move in tomorrow too, so that'll keep you busy. If you need anything...extra sheets or towels, we have some reserved for staff."

"Sounds great. Do you want me to help in the office any? I have tons of experience in bookkeeping and office management."

Shelley shook her head. "I might train you to answer the phone and take reservations, but that'll come later. When there are no guests, there are no meals. You can scrounge around for leftovers, cook something for yourself or go into town. The bunkhouse has a small kitchenette, so you'll have room to keep a few groceries. Oh, and, feel free to use the studio anytime while you're here too." She smiled. "Off the clock of course."

Melena laughed. "Of course. Thank you! I'll go see if Bob needs anything."

The phone rang. "Good deal." Shelley smiled and answered the call.

Bob showed Melena how to make coffee so she'd have fresh in the morning and put her to work preparing a vegetable tray. She helped him serve lunch then took a nap. That afternoon she hiked, then swam, and then chatted with Kidd in the corral. He showed her how to saddle and unsaddle the horses and where to stow the tack.

"I'm glad you came back," he said as they walked toward the lodge for dinner. "This place is good for the soul."

Melena smiled. "I felt that the first time I drove through the gate."

The next day she trained with Marcey and fell in love with the woman's effervescent personality. After dinner, she moved her stuff into the bunkhouse, set up her computer and updated her blog...

I'm exhausted. Pleasantly so. Though not officially on the clock yet, I folded a ton of laundry—found the chore soothing. The quiet hum of washers and dryers proved the perfect, subtle background noise. Very conducive to praying. I even took a swim this afternoon and spent some time in the studio, then sat on the porch and watched the sun set in a glorious display of colors so breathtaking it made my throat close.

She uploaded a couple of photos.

Just look at these gorgeous, deep purple and magenta hues! They bleed through the sky at sunset, weeping their tint across the jutting rocks. These pictures don't even come close to doing justice to this scene. If there was ever a doubt God existed, the beauty of His creation here in this place erases it.

She signed off, then curled up on the love seat in the tiny living area with her journal—

I've been reading books on spirituality (not religion) and am amazed at how Scripture has opened up for me. I'm learning to quiet my thoughts and listen, really listen, to the voice of the Lord. I still hear Jon's voice, though not quite as clearly on some days compared to others. Maybe he is at peace knowing I'm doing something, making an effort, at least, to keep going.

Learning to live again is killing me.

Sounds like a country and western song, I know, a corny one at that, but so true. I have no idea what I'm doing or why.

And my heart weeps.

Haven't seen Garrett yet. I keep telling myself he is not the reason I'm here, but...just between us...he is part of the reason. I've never met a man so...heck, I don't even have words to describe him. LOL!

So…larger than life, so vibrant, so full of joy, so bright of spirit. Have no idea what it is about him that intrigues me.

Melena chewed on the end of her pen. She hadn't meant to delve into the paradox of emotions she had toward Garrett, but now that she'd given a voice to them, she couldn't stop the memory of the first time they met from crowding her thoughts. She recalled the incidents when their eyes met or hands touched, seemingly by accident, in the time she'd been at the retreat. And though he'd given equal attention to all of the guests, especially those of the female persuasion, she couldn't help but wonder if the sparks between them were mutual or one-sided. *Guess time will tell.*

"Doesn't matter," she said aloud and snapped the journal shut. "I'm here for me." Determined to put him out of her mind, she picked up the book she was currently enjoying and read another chapter, making notes and highlighting passages that truly spoke to her. When her mind fogged and eyes began to droop, she set that aside, went into the bedroom and said her evening prayers. She fell into a deep, dreamless slumber. The first of many restful nights to come.

Chapter Seven

Melena awoke groggy and heavy-headed from a night wrought with despair.

Nine months today.

Her breath hitched. A wave of pain washed over and through her. She curled up into a tiny ball and wept. A knock sounded on the bunkhouse door. Kidd's voice came through the thin wood.

"Melena?"

She stumbled to the door and fumbled with the knob.

He took one look and stepped through, arms open.

Melena buried her face in his chest and sobbed. "It...it's b—been nine m—m—months today."

"I'll tell Shelley you won't be in."

"Oh, that's right, I'm supposed to work with Bob today. I don't want to leave anyone in a bind."

"Don't worry, we got'cha covered."

Melena shook her head. "Tell them I'll be down in a minute."

"You sure?"

"Yeah, beats the heck out of staying up here and crying all day."

Kidd left. Melena took a shower, dabbed a little concealer under her eyes and stumbled down to the lodge. Shelley met her when she walked in the staff entrance through the laundry room.

"Kidd says you're having a rough day?"

Melena managed to blink back the deluge and nod.

"Marcey's switched with you. She'll help Bob in the kitchen and serve guests. You can clean rooms and do laundry."

Gratitude swelled in her breast. "Oh, thank you!"

Shelley smiled and gave her a hug. "Not a problem. We all know you're going through a tough time, and we want to help as much as possible. You might see if they need you to wash the dishes or something later, stay behind the scenes, so to speak. If things get too rough, take the day off."

Melena shook her head. "Oh, no, this is great. Thanks again. I'll check with Marcey and Bob at lunch about the dishes."

"Great. Here's the master key. Marcey showed you how to fill out the board and flip room cards in the office, right?"

Melena nodded.

"Okay then, see you at lunch time. Oh, I think there are sheets in the dryer. You might start with that, so they don't get too wrinkled."

"Will do." Melena thanked her again as Shelley exited the room. She pulled sheets out of the dryer and laid them across the folding table then transferred more from the washer. She lifted a sheet, mated the ends and snapped it into shape. Garrett strolled through the door, a whistle on his lips, as she was folding it in half.

"Mornin'." He maneuvered around her to punch his card into the time clock.

"Hi."

"Ooh, sounds like someone had a rough night. Hung over?"

Melena glanced over her shoulder and shook her head. Sympathy filled his gaze and he turned a pale shade of embarrassed. He inched around her this time and ran a hand over her shoulder. Heat trailed in its wake. She resisted the urge to fling herself in his arms and beg him to hold her. They stood a full moment, eyes locked, then he took a step back.

"Sorry." He escaped to the corral.

Melena put the laundry she'd folded away, grabbed the cleaning supplies, loaded the cart and went out to a set of four cabins away from the main lodge. There she allowed the gamut of emotions to run their course. Prayer combined with scrubbing created a healthy outlet, and she felt better by the time she completed her task and returned to the lodge. Once again, she transferred laundry from washer to dryer, then folded and put away what needed to be. After marking the housekeeping board, she went into the office to flip cards on those rooms, showing them unoccupied and clean.

Lunchtime rolled around and she ate her meal in the kitchen while Bob and Marcey served guests, and then stayed to wash dishes. Afterward, she went upstairs to the rooms that needed to be cleaned within the lodge. By the time she clocked out, she felt purged. And exhausted.

In the bunkhouse, she showered, and then decided to ride into town and sightsee. A stone's throw from Boerne, Austin, and San Antonio, as well as Bandera—a huge tourist attraction—Utopia, known as the "paradise" of Texas Hill Country, was wildly unpopulated compared to those metropolises. B&Bs, vacation homes, and country cabins dotted the landscape amidst trees and various types of foliage native to the terrain.

The 'Lost Maples Natural Area' and a world-renowned golf course were the main attractions in and nearest to Utopia, but the variety of wildlife and birds resident to the rugged canyons and cool streams, lured people to the area year around.

She arrived back at the ranch just as guests started to gather around the wagon for the evening hayride and bonfire. Garrett waved her down.

"Coming on the hayride?"

Melena shook her head.

"Ever been on the hayride with us?"

"Not yet."

"Then come on. I'll wait for you."

She sighed. "I'm really kind of tired."

A frown creased his brow. Garrett raked a hand through his hair and adjusted his hat. "Won't take no for an answer. Park your truck and come on."

"Maybe next time." She started to ease away.

He slapped a hand on the door to halt her escape. "Melena, don't make me come after you."

She looked at him wide-eyed, then narrowed her gaze. "What did you say to me?"

His eyes lit up. That darn dimple danced in his cheek.

"It's my duty as a cowboy and a gentleman to never let a lady cry for long. You've done enough of that for one day."

How could she refuse?

Melena parked her truck, pocketed her keys and went on her very first hayride. She admired how Bill Penn wove stories around the history of the area in with feeding the longhorns. Afterward, they travelled to a nearby state natural area where the guests wandered down to a creek and skipped rocks. Melena sat on a small boulder and drew in the scent of fresh, crisp air, earth and flowers.

Sounds magnified in the pristine environment as daylight waned and dusk edged in, leeching color from the sky. The trickling of the stream as it moved across its bed. Plop, plop of stones hitting the water. A quiet laugh. The click of a camera as Garrett wove through the guests taking pictures. A bird trilled in the distance. Doves cooed. Frogs began their evening song accentuated by the occasional hoot of an owl. A hush fell over the entourage and stillness ensued.

Garrett touched her arm and pointed to a thicket across the way. Melena gasped as a doe and fawn stepped out and drank. Once the pair moved on, the group loaded back onto the hay wagon and returned to the ranch. Relaxed and happy, they congregated around the campfire area while Garrett and Bill Penn stacked wood. Soon, a fire lit up the night sky. Crickets and chickadees kept cadence with the country music provided by an outdoor stereo. Garrett brought Melena a s'more. Rich, dark chocolate and marshmallow oozed out between graham crackers.

"Thank you."

He grinned. "Aren't you glad you came along?"

She laughed. "Not that I had much choice, but yes, I'm glad."

"Much prettier with a smile on your face and a light in those sexy green eyes," he remarked, then walked over to tend to the fire.

Nerves quivered in her chest, stole her breath. Melena finished her s'more, then excused herself and escaped to the bunkhouse. The pungent odor of smoke clung to her hair and clothes, so she took another shower, donned pajamas, and then laid her garments over the porch rail to air out. She curled up in the bed with her journal...

Just as the three-and six-month marks hit hard, so did the ninth. I barely made it out of bed this morning. But by the grace of God and the compassion and understanding of the friends I've found here, I made it through another day. Another month. Now if I can get through the night...

* * * * *

Melena poured a fresh cup of coffee then went out to sit on the porch. She'd heard Kidd moving around in his part of the duplex they shared for about an hour. Any moment now, he'd be heading down to feed and gather horses for the day's guests. As though summoned by her thoughts, his door opened. She smiled over at him. "Good morning."

He tipped his hat. "Morning. Better today?"

Melena nodded. "Yeah, I made it through another night. Another month. Hard to believe it's been nine months. Sometimes it feels like yesterday, others an eternity ago. But," she shrugged, swallowed hard. "Life goes on. Unfortunately, I have no choice but to go on with it."

"Realizing that is the first of many steps toward healing."

Melena sipped her coffee. "Yeah, I just wish it weren't so difficult. Wish there weren't so many unanswered questions."

"You'll get 'em figured out. One at a time."

She sipped again, hated the way her hand shook. "Thanks for the vote of confidence."

Kidd stooped down to eye level with her. "You're a strong, beautiful, talented woman, Melena. God has great plans for your future. Don't let this tragedy, this grief, cloud that truth."

She offered a weak smile. "Yeah, so they all say. Whoever in the world 'they' are. But the one thing I can't figure out, can't wrap my mind around, is *why* or more specifically, *what*. What on earth does God have for me to do that Jon couldn't be a part of? Makes no sense to me. He was my biggest fan, my greatest supporter. He gave me strength and courage and purpose..."

She sucked in a deep, shuddering breath and lifted the cup to her mouth once more. "I'm sorry. I didn't want to do this today."

Kidd shook his head. "No need to apologize. The answers are there, Melena. And they'll be revealed to you one day. But you've got to get this grief out of the way. Now, I'm not saying that should happen in nine months, or even nine years. Well, nine years would be a little long. My point is, there's no timeframe on grieving and until you look beyond it, move past it, and open up to the possibilities, you'll never hear or see those answers."

Melena smiled. "You sound like my friend, Pat."

He chuckled. "Well, if two of us are saying the same thing, there's got to be some truth in it."

His laughter bolstered her flagging emotions. She laughed. "How come you never married again, Kidd?"

He eyed her for a long, tense moment.

"If that's none of my business, just say so. You won't hurt my feelings."

Kidd's eyes softened. He reached out and stroked the hair off her cheek. "I'm still waiting for her to come around."

Melena frowned. "That's an odd choice of words."

A quick flash of guilt lit his eyes, darkened his cheeks. Melena narrowed her gaze. "You're flirting with me while seeing someone else? Isn't that against the cowboy code of honor or something?"

The flush deepened. "No...yes..." he stuttered. "Hell. Not officially."

"What exactly does that mean?"

"It means I've been stupid. I'm not dating anyone. I've always been friendly and fun-loving but never thought how that might appear to others or impact them. You're right, it's not very gentlemanly. I'm sorry."

Melena smiled. "Apology accepted. Don't change your personality, Kidd. It's what makes you such a sweet man. Whoever she is, she'll come around. Just wait and see."

"Oh, I probably couldn't change if I wanted to. Or wouldn't if someone asked me to. But you have given me something to think about." He rose and adjusted his hat. "You working today?"

He is such a sweetie. Melena nodded.

"See you at breakfast, then." He stepped off the porch.

Melena took the last sip of her coffee and grimaced because it had grown cold. She carried her cup inside, traded it for her camera and decided to take a short walk before breakfast and work.

The sun peeked over the horizon, cast shadows on some hills, glorious hues on others. Melena snapped pictures, envisioned them transferred onto canvas or glass. The breakfast bell rang, and she hurried to put her camera away and eat before she had to clock in. She hadn't thought of the incident with Kidd until he and Garrett strolled into the dining area, piled food on a plate, and pulled out a chair beside her at the staff table, fondly called "the circle of love."

"Have a nice walk?" he asked.

Melena lifted a glass of orange juice to her lips and nodded.

"I saw you out with your camera. Get some good shots?" Garrett wanted to know.

She put the glass down. "Got some great pics, can't wait to get into the studio."

Marcey served the last guest and joined them just as Melena finished her statement.

"If you want to take the day off, I can handle the workload. Not much to do after flipping the two rooms in one of the cabins for the guests checking into them this afternoon."

Marcey was a single mom and this, her only source of income. Melena had no desire to infringe on the permanent staff's time or money. She smiled. "Thanks, Marcey. I'd love to do that."

They laughed and talked the remainder of the meal. Afterward, she and Marcey washed dishes and helped Bob clean the kitchen. They gathered the cleaning supplies and linens, then went out to the cabin.

"So what's going on with you and Kidd?" Marcey asked as they stripped and remade beds.

Melena flushed, stuttered, and then emitted a self-conscious little chuckle. "Well, considering he's young enough to be my son, nothing's going on. Why do you ask?"

Marcey shrugged. "He just gets a certain gleam in his eye when he looks at you. Come to think of it, so does Garrett. Any news there?"

This time Melena laughed, surprised at the intense surge of emotions at the mere suggestion of her and Garrett as an item. "Now, there's a cowboy for you, but no, nothing's going on between us either. Both are sweet as they can be, very supportive and kind, and great dance partners, but that's the extent of our relationships. What about you, have your eye on any one in particular?"

Marcey rolled her eyes with a snort. "No cowboy for me. Been there, done that, burned the t-shirt. I want someone who is settled and responsible. Most cowboys aren't." She smiled and there was no mistaking the light of friendship and respect in her gaze. "Take it from me, guard your heart. Especially when it comes to those two."

Melena swallowed the emotion that rose to clog her throat. "Kind of hard not to like them, care about them even, but my heart is still bound."

Marcey's eyes softened. "I can't imagine loving someone that much. Or being loved like that in return."

Longing colored her tone. Melena stepped around the bed and enfolded the younger woman in her embrace. "Then open your mind and broaden your horizons, Marcey. Otherwise you're settling for less than God's best."

Marcey sighed. "Been in so many screwed-up relationships it's pathetic. My man-picker isn't all that sharp. Guess I ought to just forget about one altogether."

Melena tucked the sheets then tugged the comforter into place. "What's your idea of a perfect man?"

Marcey shrugged. "Someone honest and faithful and responsible."

"Pretty broad spectrum, there. What about looks, personality?"

Marcey thought a moment then shrugged again. "Looks and personality aren't everything. It's character I want. And integrity."

"Those are great qualities, but Marcey...unless you're specific about what kind of man you want, you won't know him when you meet him."

"What do you mean?"

Melena paused in her task, thought, prayed. "I've been reading a lot of spiritual books, not about other religions, but about a new way, a different level, of thinking and praying. One of them talks about how God answers specific prayer. Think about the men you've known, the father…"

"Fathers," Marcey corrected.

Melena nodded. "Okay, the fathers of your children. What was the thing about each you loved the most? Write that down. Then think about what quality they lacked and write that down too. Then imagine you could create the perfect man for yourself. Really think hard and pray, then write that down as well."

"Sounds kind of weird and like the new age mumbo-jumbo going around."

Melena laughed. "Maybe a little, but I believe it's more about clarity. If we can't be clear about what we want, how can we expect God to bless us with it? Now I know He's omnipresent and omnipotent, and He knows what's best for us, but He does give us the freedom of choice and individuality. I mean, think about it. If you were going to redecorate a room, wouldn't you consider every aspect? Paint, curtains, floors?"

Marcey nodded.

"Everybody's different and unique in their wants and desires, especially when it comes to picking spouses. If you're not specific in what you truly, deep down want in a partner, you'll just keep getting bits and pieces of your ideal mate in different packages."

"Wow, I never thought about it like that."

Melena smiled. "Most of us don't. I remember as a child dreaming about my knight in shining armor…what he would look like, what he would do for a living, where we'd live, how many kids we'd have. I never wavered from that idea, those qualities, and he was always the same, every time I thought about him or described him to my friends. Jon was everything I'd ever dreamed of and then some. So, you see, there's got to be something spiritual, something credible in being specific."

They finished the room, moved into the adjoining one and continued their conversation.

"You think that works in looks too?"

Melena laughed. "I don't know. I wanted tall, dark and handsome. Jon was medium height and build and I've seen better-looking men. But he took my breath away and he treated me like a queen. The way he honored our vows made love, honor and respect a joy instead of the job most people claim them to be. He was funny and kind, sweet and romantic, respectful and honest and faithful. And very sentimental."

"Sounds like the perfect man to me."

Melena smiled. "Oh, he wasn't perfect. Had his faults, as anyone else does, but he had my love and affection, and I had his. And we never let each other forget that, never took it for granted."

"Sounds like you two had the kind of relationship most people only dream about."

Melena wiped the wetness from her cheeks, surprised the sharp stab of grief wasn't as intense as it was yesterday. "We did. But we had that kind of relationship because we worked at it. We took time out every day for each other. Time to talk, plan, and dream. Instead of murmuring and complaining about each other's faults, we built each other up. Love is kind of like a garden. If you don't take the time to plant, water and nurture, nothing good will grow."

"Well, I certainly wish you peace and happiness again. I know it's hard on you. Not that I've been there. But it shows in your eyes. Even when you smile there's a sadness in them. Seems better since you came back to work, especially when we're all out at the club."

Melena considered a moment before she answered. "There's something special about this place. Peace and healing in these hills. I love dancing. It helps me forget the pain, if only for a little while."

Once the rooms were clean, Marcey opted to walk so Melena drove the cart back to the lodge, unloaded it, transferred laundry from washer to dryer and put two more loads on to wash. Then she went into the office to speak with Shelley, who gave her the rest of the afternoon off. Melena drove into town and printed out the photos she'd taken that morning, then grabbed a bite of lunch before returning to the ranch. Once there, she escaped into the studio.

Chapter Eight

Melena sat back on the stool, amazed and humbled at what had come out of her, through her. Collages on canvas, shadows on silk, glitter on glass. Not just one of the numerous photos spread out on the corkboard behind her easel, but a compilation of many, transposed onto different surfaces in various dimensions. Her hands shook as she cleaned the workspace and brushes. Turpentine stung the tiny cuts she received while shaping the glass art, so wrapped up in the moment she hadn't even noticed. She glanced at the projects again, overwhelmed.

"Oh, God," she whispered. She closed her eyes and let emotion shiver through. "I had no idea I was even capable of such beauty. Thank You for this gift, this talent. May I always use it to glorify You."

A knock interrupted her prayer. "Yes?"

The door cracked open. "Melena?"

"Come on in, Kidd."

He stepped through the door. "You sure it's okay? I know most artists don't want to be disturbed or their work interrupted, much less seen before it's complete."

She laughed. "I'm finished for today."

He walked to where she sat, glanced around. A low wolf whistle sounded in his throat. "Looks like you've found your calling." He sent her a somber look. "Don't forget us little people when you're rich and famous."

Tiny bubbles of heat burst beneath her skin. Melena smiled, cocked her head and tried to see the work through his eyes. "What makes you think I've got what it takes to be rich and famous? I've seen much better art than this."

"I haven't. Been working here three years now and, out of all the artists that've come through, none can hold a candle to you. Wait until Bill or Anne sees this. You'll be on your way to stardom in no time."

On impulse, Melena hugged him. "Thank you, Kidd."

The moment shifted. He put his arms around her waist, turned his head so their lips were a breath apart. His eyes softened, darkened.

A tremble skittered along her spine. *He's testing me. Or maybe himself.* Melena took a step back before he could kiss her. Rejection flickered in his eyes, shadowed his features. "I guess I should apologize, especially after our conversation this morning."

Her pulse stuttered. Her flesh burned where he'd touched. Melena shook her head. "No...Kidd...it's me...I..." She fisted a hand in the hem of her shirt, closed her eyes and fought the tremors his nearness invoked. "Good grief, Kidd. My son is almost thirty years old. You can't be much older than him."

He chuckled and took a step back. "Got a few years on him."

Melena breathed easier with even that minute distance between them. "I don't want things to be awkward between us."

Kidd adjusted his hat. "Neither do I, but I can't pretend I'm not attracted to you."

Melena took a deep, trembling breath. "I'm flattered. Honestly. I'm just not ready for anything more than friendship."

Understanding lit his gaze. A relieved smile curved her lips. "Besides, I gathered this morning that although you're not *officially...*" she finger-quoted the word for emphasis, "dating anyone, you do have someone in mind."

He sighed. "Man gets tired of waiting, tired of getting the brush-off." He turned on his heel and walked to the door. Waited. "Dinner's getting cold."

"I'll be down in a minute."

He nodded, walked through and closed the door behind him.

Melena dropped down onto the stool once more. *Oh my.*

Moments later someone else knocked on the studio door. "Come on in." Melena ran trembling hands over cold, wet cheeks.

Anne Penn stepped through. "You have a phone call in the office, Melena."

Melena rose, her first thoughts of fear. They must have shown on her face. Anne touched her arm.

"Not an emergency, just your friend Pat wanting to speak with you. Kidd said you had some pretty awesome work in here. Mind if I take a look while you have your conversation?"

Melena shook her head. "Not at all."

"Okay, I'll meet you in the dining room."

Melena hurried down and answered the phone. "Hello?"

"How are you?"

"I'm really good. What's up?"

Pat chuckled. "Oh, nothing. No one talked to you yesterday and you didn't update your blog or email, so I got wrangled into calling to check on you."

Melena laughed. "Yesterday was hellacious, today a rollercoaster, but I made it through."

"Good. So, how's it working out, Mel? Really? I follow your posts and your emails sound as though you're having a good time."

"I am, Pat. It's so delightful here. Everyone is supportive, giving me room to grieve when I need it then always making me laugh when the crying jag is over. The past couple of weeks have been such fun and I've settled into a routine with the crew. I actually like the work. Not much different from what I've done all these years as a wife and mother, just on a larger scale. One thing I've found most soothing is horseback riding."

"Seriously?" Pat interjected.

Melena laughed. "Yeah. Who would have guessed, right? Me, a city girl from the word go, up on a horse and enjoying it! But I do. Nothing is quite as soothing as the gentle clip-clop of hooves on rock. Guess I need to call everyone and check in."

"No need. I'll fill them in."

"Yeah, but I haven't gone this long without talking to Karyn since the day she was born. I just couldn't handle it yesterday. You know? The weight of grief sits so heavy on me, especially when I hear it in her voice, their voices."

"That's understandable, Mel, but kids are resilient. I visited with Kathryn and her family for quite a while this morning and Karyn is fine. They all are, really. Just concerned because they hadn't heard from you. Karyn loves following your blog and seeing the photos you post. She gets a kick out of reading your emails too. It's just as effective as a phone call. Maybe more so, because she can keep looking at it, reread them. Makes the distance less daunting, your presence, and your love more tangible. So just keep that up. I'm so glad you're doing better."

Melena sighed. "It's amazing, Pat, like this whole new world has opened up to me. I mean, the sights, the sounds, the colors. My art is going really well, too. I've even astounded myself. It's exhilarating and scary all at once."

Pat chuckled. "Life can be that way. Look, I'm going to get off now and let you go. I'll call your kids and parents and fill them in and I'll see you in a couple of weeks."

"You're coming up?"

"Yeah. Ms. Penn didn't tell you?"

"No."

"I've booked a room for week after next."

"That's wonderful! I can't wait to see you. Tell everyone I'll call tomorrow. I love you, Pat. See you soon."

They hung up just as Anne Penn walked into the office. "Have a nice chat?"

Melena smiled and nodded.

"I'd like to talk with you about your work. Have you eaten?"

Melena shook her head. "Not yet. Got sidetracked."

Anne laughed. "Well, let's go get you a plate before it's all picked up and we'll talk."

Melena followed her into the dining area. Anne refreshed her glass of tea and got one for Melena while Melena filled a plate and gathered silverware. They sat at the staff table alone, as the rest of the employees were off tending to various duties.

Melena paused and said a silent prayer over her food then took a bite. A satisfied little hum sounded in her throat. "The food here is always so delicious."

Anne laughed. "Bob is an artist in his own right. That's why we keep him around."

Melena smiled. "He does manage to create delicious meals around the same ingredients."

"Well, the guests usually want ranch-type fare, but they all love Bob's cooking." Anne waited a beat, continued only after Melena swallowed the bite she'd just taken.

"How would you feel about us hosting an art show for you in the fall?"

Melena's eyes widened. "Are you serious?"

Anne smiled and nodded. "Very. Every now and then an artist comes through here that we feel could use a boost with his or her career. The work I examined in the studio is a higher caliber than I've seen in a long time. We'd like to sponsor your career."

Melena put her fork down. "Wow. I knew it was good, but..." Her words trailed off as the magnitude of Anne's words sank in. "Sponsor my career? What does that mean?"

"We'll host a show for you this fall in conjunction with the annual fair the town puts on, introduce you to people we know who understand and buy fine art, set up a gallery tour if you'd like. There are a number of things we could do with and for you."

Melena gasped. "My goodness, I never dreamed this would happen. I mean, art has always been a hobby for me. A joy and pleasure I indulged in, but never in my wildest imagination did I believe I was good enough for all that. I mean... I have no idea what's going to happen when the summer is over, where I'll be or what I'll do. What if I can't create like this at home…? What if I have to go back to work at the end of this year…? What if I can't keep up?"

She pressed trembling fingers to her lips as possibilities and fears warred in her mind. "Oh, listen to me ramble and I didn't even thank you for the compliment."

Anne laughed and patted her hand. "Don't worry about all that right now. We don't need all the answers this moment." She rose from the table, placed her hand on Melena's shoulder, and gave a light squeeze. "Take some time to think and pray. But if you'd like to do the show, I'll need to start promoting it soon."

Melena nodded. Anne turned away, took a few steps toward the office. Melena drew a deep breath and listened to the voices inside urging her to take a leap of faith…Jon's, Pat's and the One she'd come to know so intimately in the last few months. "Anne?"

Anne hesitated, turned back to face her.

"Can we start with the show and go from there?"

Anne's smile lit up her entire face. "Sure can."

Melena took the plunge before she had a chance to chicken out. "Then let's do it."

"Great! I'll start putting some information together. We'll need a bio on you and pictures of your work."

"What do I need to do?"

Anne laughed. "Spend as many hours in the studio as you feel led. We're pretty booked this weekend, so you won't have much time. Next week isn't as full. I'll talk to Shelley about your schedule. We can give Marcey a few more hours in order for you to have time off. We'll get together toward the end of the week to finalize brochures and advertising material."

"I didn't realize there was so much work involved."

Anne shook her head. "Not for you to worry about. All you need to do is focus on creating your masterpiece."

"Masterpiece?"

Anne nodded. "At some point you'll create a single piece of art that we'll use to build the entire show around. Something that speaks to the soul—yours and everyone who gazes upon it. Don't worry, it'll come naturally, and you'll know from the moment it's finished. Eat now, before your food gets too cold."

She spun on her heel and disappeared into the office.

Eat? Melena pressed a hand to her quivering stomach. *Oh, God, what have I agreed to?* She pushed the food around on her plate. Her stomach kneaded the few bites she managed to get past her constricted throat. Exasperated, she scraped the remains into the trash, rinsed her dishes and went to the bunkhouse.

* * * * *

The weekend passed in a flurry of activity, and Melena didn't have a single moment to spare for the studio, much less worry over the upcoming show or creating a masterpiece. She did however, file ideas for future work into a corner of her mind. She tucked away the sights, sounds and emotions experienced over five full days of guests coming and going: children's laughter, sunshine, sparkling water, firelight, glittering stars, lightning bugs, and the glow of a full moon. She worked harder in those few days than she had in all the years she spent behind a desk.

Each day, or evening, before or after her shift, she sketched and colored and took photographs. She visited with the artists that came through on tours or a weekend retreat. By the time her first day off rolled around, she was too exhausted to do anything but relax by the pool or in the sauna and hot tub. But her mind swam with ideas. Her fingers itched to paint and mold.

The next day, she climbed the stairs to the studio to find her regular spot empty, all of her work missing.

She rushed down the stairs and into the office. Her breath came in jagged pants, and her heart threatened to leap from her chest. "It's gone."

Anne rose from her desk. "Whoa, what are you talking about?"

"My work. Everything I've done over the past month. Disappeared." Her words hitched on a sob.

Anne shook her head. "No, it's not. I moved everything into a private studio so nothing would get damaged or copied or stolen."

Every ounce of oxygen whooshed out of her lungs. Her knees buckled. She slumped down in a chair and clutched the arms until the shudders stopped and her frantic pulse returned to normal. Overwhelmed in the aftermath of emotions, she trembled. Sobs rendered her words mere stutter. "I n—never thought of that. I—th—thought I'd l—lost ev—ery—th—thing. Again."

Anne gathered Melena in her arms, patted her back. "I'm sorry, we've been so crazy busy, I didn't get a chance to tell you."

When the turmoil subsided, Melena apologized.

Anne patted her hand. "It's okay. I should have thought to leave a note or something."

Melena took a deep, cleansing inhale and attempted a smile to ease the embarrassment winding through the relief. "Whew, didn't know I had all that pent-up emotion in there."

Anne chuckled. "Glad I could be of service to help you get rid of it." She sobered. "Are you sure you're okay?"

Melena sighed. "I've been teetering on the edge of okay for more than a year now if you count the months Jon was ill, but yeah, I feel better now than I did when I first ran down here like a crazy woman."

Anne laughed with her. "Good." She handed Melena a key and told her where the studio was located. "Keep this with you and lock up when you leave. It's for your exclusive use until the show."

Melena slid the key into her pocket. "I haven't been able to work—well, to paint or do glass—but I have a dozen or more sketches, photographs and ideas."

Anne nodded. "Good. Have you thought about a theme?"

Melena shook her head. "Not really."

"Well, don't worry over it, something will come to you. Usually when you least expect it."

Bill Penn hesitated in the doorway, then stepped through the office entry. Melena watched the interplay of emotions on Anne's face and sighed. She smiled. "Kind of like love, huh?"

"Yep, when you least expect it." Anne lifted her cheek to receive her husband's greeting.

Melena slipped out of her chair and left them alone. She went into the private studio tucked away in an alcove on the third floor of the lodge, surprised to find her work arranged in an attractive display. Direct light shone on some, muted on others.

Melena wandered around the room. Her gaze rested on each

individual piece of art, amazed again at what God had seen fit to express through her.

Her easel stood in the center of the room. She made her way to the stool and sat. Her mind whirled with visions, yet she hesitated to put images to paper. She closed her eyes and heard the voice of her art instructor from years past.

"What do you see? What do you feel? Delve deeper."

One word came to mind, echoed in her spirit. *Serenity*.

Melena rose, wandered around the room once more and gazed upon her creations with a new set of eyes.

The eyes of her spirit.

She tugged on frames, readjusted light, and rearranged pieces until her theme fell into place.

Serenity.

She placed a fresh canvas on the easel, filled her palette with color, mixed shades and, with soft strokes of the brush, painted.

Chapter Nine

Melena sprayed degreaser on the table, swiped a clean cloth over it, moved on to the next and tried to keep her excitement at bay. Pat was due to arrive any minute now.

Though she wasn't on the clock, and since she couldn't sit still long enough to paint, she cleaned and folded laundry to keep her hands and mind busy. Between the constant ebb and flow of guests, her time in the studio, and work, the last two weeks had flown by. Now, she could hardly wait to see her friend.

She'd talked to her children and grandchildren and everyone wondered when she would be home. "Soon," she'd say, but cringed at the mere thought of returning to that empty house. Empty life.

Melena closed her eyes and took a deep breath. One day at a time, she told herself. Relax, live, laugh, learn, grow and be happy today. Let tomorrow take care of itself and deal with going home when the time comes.

She finished wiping tables and straightening chairs then swept the dining room. She'd put away the cleaning supplies and washed her hands when she heard the front door of the lodge open and close. She rushed out and flew into her friend's arms, laughing and crying at once.

Pat stepped out of Melena's embrace and held her an arm's length away. "Look at you, you look fabulous!"

Melena emitted a self-conscious giggle and smoothed a hand over her hair. "The physical work's been good for me. That and swimming—along with my daily walk, not to mention dancing several nights a week, have really helped by toning muscles I'd forgotten about."

She hugged Pat again. "You look wonderful as always. How was your trip?"

Pat sighed. "Long but lovely. You're right, I've seen a lot of places in the world but there is something special about this Hill Country. I felt it the moment I headed north. Girl, we've *got* to visit Bandera while I'm here."

Melena chuckled. "I'm off the entire time you're in so we'll make a trip down there. Spend the day."

Pat's wriggled her eyebrows and grinned. "The day my foot. More like a couple of days. I've got to see if it truly is 'the cowboy capital of the world,' as they claim."

Melena laughed. "Wait until you see my cowboys."

"Your cowboys?"

Melena's chin lifted at the teasing edge to Pat's voice. Her flesh warmed. "That's right, *my* cowboys. They are both adorable and I love them to pieces."

No sooner had the words left Melena's mouth when the objects of her affection walked in from the kitchen. Both men stopped, glanced at each other and grinned. Then they tipped their hats in Pat's direction with a simultaneous, "Ma'am."

Pat hummed a little "oh my" then nodded in response to their greeting. "Gentlemen."

Melena fought down a surge of jealous irritation at the blatant charm, laid on thick by the two men as they fumbled over each other in an effort to serve Pat. Garrett offered to bring in her luggage while Kidd suggested he get her a drink. Pat handed Garrett her keys and asked Kidd for a diet cola. Both scrambled to please while Melena scolded herself. *Stop it! You might call them your cowboys but neither belongs to you.*

"Thank God," she muttered.

Pat eyed her, a curious lift to her brow. Melena's cheeks grew warm. "Sorry, off in a world of my own."

Pat laughed and crooked her arm through Melena's. "True cowboy etiquette."

Melena rolled her eyes. "True cowboy ego. I swear you'd think we were in high school and you the new girl in town."

Pat's gaze narrowed even as her lips twitched. "Why, Mel, I do believe your eyes are a little greener than I remember."

Melena realized her own reaction was as high schoolish as the guys'. She flushed and tried to come up with a response, stuttered instead, and then simply burst into wild laughter with her friend.

"Let's drive them crazy," Pat suggested in a conspiratorial whisper.

Melena giggled. "Okay, but only a little. I'll still be living and working here once you've escaped."

"Can't have no fun in Utopia, Texas." Pat groaned in exaggerated disappointment then laughed with Melena. "When is the next scheduled night out on the town? I could definitely use a waltz or two across a sawdust-covered floor, especially after that drive," she remarked as Kidd placed her drink on the table and Garrett strolled in pulling her suitcase.

Kidd glanced at his watch. "We'd be happy to escort you ladies on your quest and much obliged to twirl you across the dance floor a time or two. Right, Garrett?"

"You bet," Garrett agreed.

Pat eyed Melena. "You game, Mel?"

Melena shrugged. "If that's what you want to do."

"We're here to serve, huh, Mel?" Garrett interjected with a hint of emphasis on her nickname.

Those mesmerizing blue eyes sparkled with mirth, dimple winked. Pat's suggestion to drive them crazy ran through her mind. Melena shook her head and narrowed her gaze at him. "You don't have permission to call me that." She whirled on Kidd. "Neither do you."

"Why not?" Both wanted to know.

Pat leaned over and slung an arm around Melena's neck then pulled her to where they were cheek to cheek. "'Cause you don't know her well enough."

Kidd scraped back his chair and stood. "Been trying to remedy that," he mumbled, then chuckled when Melena turned several shades of red.

Pat arched a brow at him. "Really?" She stood and slipped her arm through his. "Pray tell."

Garrett leaned over as the two strolled toward the door. "How hard has he tried and how close has he gotten?"

Melena's heart tripped over itself at the intimate tone and soft gaze. The idea of frivolous flirting with these two had a sudden sharp edge to it. A plethora of adjectives swam through her head...*innocent, fun*...daring. Excitement curled through her. She let the question hang until anticipation shimmered. Her lips curved. She shrugged, pushed away from the table, and left the answer dangling between them.

Thirty minutes later the foursome arrived at the nearest hot spot and the fun began. Pat determined to dance with every cowboy in the place. Not to be outdone, Melena promised to do the same. They laughed and talked, danced and flirted and placed bets on who—between Kidd and Garrett—would have the worst hangover. Kidd seemed to know instinctively which songs would render Melena a helpless mass of emotion as guilt nipped at her mind and sorrow gnawed on her conscience. At the first notes of each tear-jerker, he came to the rescue by pulling her out on the dance floor.

Whirling her across the sawdust, he gazed down at her with a tender smile. "No crying, Mel."

She buried her face against his shoulder. "Jon and Pat are the only two people who were ever allowed to call me Mel."

He grinned. "What does it take to be given the privilege?"

A lifetime of devotion. Melena swallowed the retort. If she wasn't careful, the glint in his eyes and tone of his voice would be her undoing. The song ended before he could press her for an answer. She thanked him and escaped into the ladies' room. Pat met her in there.

"You okay?"

Melena nodded. "Yeah, just some songs are harder to listen to than others. Added to the wine coolers and exhaustion, I'm about done in."

"We can leave whenever you're ready," Pat said.

Melena shook her head. "No. Tonight is all about you. I'll be fine, just need a minute."

Pat hugged her. "Okay, but if you're not out before the next song ends, I'll send Kidd or Garrett in here after you."

Melena laughed.

Pat touched her shoulder. "You look really well, Melena. It does me good to see you smile and hear you laugh. And it *is* okay for you to do so."

Melena splashed water on her face. "I know. I'm getting there."

"Good! Now let's go find a cowboy to waltz across Texas with."

They walked out of the bathroom and right into her cowboys' arms. Kidd twirled Pat once then eased into a waltz with her. Garrett pulled Melena close and maneuvered her onto the floor. He bent his head and the warmth of his breath caressed her ear.

"So, you never did answer my question."

"What question?"

He pulled her a notch closer, and another, until Melena found herself plastered against his hard chest.

"How hard has Kidd tried to get to know you, and how close has he gotten?"

Melena eased back. "About the same as you."

Garrett's jaw hardened. He flashed a narrowed gaze over her head then back to lock with hers. "Guess I'll have to work harder."

Before she could respond, he twirled and spun her around the floor until she clung to him for dear life.

* * * * *

Melena sat on her stool in the studio while Pat walked around and examined the work she had produced over the last month. She knew her friend supported her talent but never in her wildest dreams did she imagine the admiration in Pat's eyes when she turned after studying the masterpiece Melena finished two days ago.

"Mel. This is...fabulous."

Melena flushed.

Pat closed her eyes and took a deep breath. "I knew you were talented, but this..." She turned back to the painting and glasswork, shook her head. "This is more than I *ever* dreamed you were capable of."

Emotions shivered through Melena when awe filled her friend's gaze.

"This is it, Mel. This is what God has called you to do. This is why you're still here. Among other reasons of course. I feel deep in my spirit He is going to use you in ways you never dreamed or imagined."

Pleasure and pain washed through Melena. "Maybe so, Pat, but I still don't understand why Jon had to go. I mean, he was my greatest supporter. He always encouraged me and gave me the time and space I needed when I did make the effort to work on my art."

"Yes, but would Jon have allowed you to come away like this? Would you have *wanted* to? I'm not asking that to make you doubt yourself, him, or your love for each other, but Mel, examine your life and ask yourself those questions. God has a reason and a plan for each of us. Art is so obviously a part of His plan for you, and I think if you really open up to the possibilities, there are no limits to where He will take you. Take your career."

Agony twisted Melena's chest as memories of years past flitted through her mind. Jon may have allowed her the freedom of expression in her art. He supported her, even encouraged her to pursue her craft, but truth of the matter was he wanted her with him more than he understood her need to be away so she could do that. And, truth of the matter is, she loved him more than she loved her gift. She'd have given up, *gave up*, anything and everything for Jon. Even a part of herself.

And, she'd give it all up again just to have him back.

Liquid pooled in her eyes, rolled slowly down her cheeks. "I n—never th—thought a—about it like that," she stammered.

Pat enfolded her in a fierce embrace. "That truth doesn't diminish what you two shared, Mel. Please don't let it. What it does, is open you to the possibilities. I mean, you're at a point in your life where you have responsibilities to no one but yourself and the talent God has gifted you with. Sure, you have your family and things may arise where you need to be home and take care of them. But until those things come up, you need to focus on you and you alone. And make sure you don't run to the rescue for every little crisis.

"You raised your kids to be strong, independent, productive members of society. Let them be so, and let God take you places you've never dreamed of going. Enjoy this next phase of your life. You'll always miss Jon and part of you will probably mourn that loss forever, but don't let it hinder your destiny. I know your greatest desire was to be a wife and mother. God honored that. Now He's calling you into *His* greater plan for you."

"But what if the show this fall doesn't do as well as everyone thinks? What if I can't continue creating like this once I'm home? What if..." Melena's words trailed off when Pat gave her a slight shake.

"Don't do that! Do *not* worry about things God has under control!

You're thinking only painting and glass, but Mel, there is so much more to art. There's writing and speaking and teaching. Think outside the box."

Melena shook her head. "I cringe at the thought of public speaking and I sure as heck can't write."

Pat's eyebrow arched. "Oh, yes, you can. I've read your blogs. You have a way with words that I can't even fathom. Go back and read your own writing and think of the doors of opportunity it may open. Like a river, artistic talent runs deep. And, like any river, it has many facets. I mean, think about it. You had a wonderful marriage, one most people only dream of having. How many ways can you use that experience and what you're learning and discovering now, to help others? Books, talks with women's groups, ministries, and yes, painting and glass. Don't limit yourself."

Melena laughed. "You sure you don't want to manage my career?"

Pat grinned. "I doubt I could do you justice, but I'm sure the Penns can steer you in the right direction. Haven't they both created written work around their art?"

Melena nodded.

"Then talk to them and listen to what they say. Just don't give too much away. Have you signed anything with them yet?"

"Just a basic contract for the art show. They get fifteen percent of everything that sells."

"Have you researched that to see if it's fair?"

Melena shook her head. "Not really. I trust them."

Pat shook her head and sighed. "Trusting is all fine, good, and well but don't be naive when it comes to business. Research. Fifteen percent sounds fair but be careful of fine print and hidden clauses. You might consider having a lawyer check over any and every contract that comes your way."

Melena giggled. "Now you sound like my son."

Pat laughed. "There you go." She slid her arm through Melena's and they walked out of the studio and down the stairs. "If you feel inspired while I'm here, don't hesitate to leave me a note or something and disappear into the twilight zone."

"I will not! Inspiration will come again. You're only here for a week so I'm all yours. Besides, we have a trip to Bandera planned."

Pat heaved a lusty sigh. "Yeah, the cowboy capital of the world. Oh, my."

They reached the dining room just as Garrett walked in. His eyes swept over them in an appreciative gesture. His lips curved, dimple creased his cheek like a smile of its own. He tipped his hat.

"Ladies." He greeted them and continued on his way.

Pat turned to Melena, her eyebrow arched in speculation. "Speaking of cowboys..."

Melena flushed under the scrutiny in her gaze. "What?"

Pat's eyes narrowed. "Be careful with those two. There's not an ounce of permanency in either of their DNA."

The skin on Melena's neck and face heated. "We're just friends."

Pat snorted. "Yeah, for now. I see the way they look at you."

Melena rolled her eyes. "The same way they look at every woman, married or single, that walks in this place."

Pat nodded. "My point exactly. Guard your heart, Melena. You can't afford the kind of pain those two could bring you."

"I'll tell you like I've told Marcey—my heart is still bound."

"For now. But the day may come when your body overrules everything. That's normal and nothing to be ashamed of. But if, and I know that's a huge *if*, you decide to act on that, don't mix physical pleasure with love and commitment. The two are not always exclusive."

Melena's cheeks grew hot again. "I—"

Pat cut off her protests with a wave. "Never say never, Melena. You're an attractive, healthy woman. You're not immune to, nor hardened against, the kind of charm those two have in abundance. You're in a vulnerable place right now and you've always been soft-hearted and romantic when it comes to sex and relationships. That's okay too, but for some folks, enjoying one doesn't mean you have to be committed to the other for life."

Melena gasped. "That is so against the Bible. Of course, you've always been more liberal than me."

Pat winced. "I know, and I hadn't intended to get into this conversation with you right now, but someone's got to look after you."

She took a breath, walked over to the drink station and poured them cups of tea, then hooked her arm through Melena's and led her up the stairs and into her room before she continued. "I don't think of myself as liberal, Mel—not in the fullest sense of the word—but I do believe God is bigger than the boxes we put Him in. *Especially* those outlined in the Bible.

"I've said this before and I'll say it again, I believe the Bible is the inspired word of God, but it is written by man, filtered through man's mindsets, man's prejudices, and *man's* cultural beliefs. Heck, it has been translated so many times, there's not a bit of telling what is in the original texts and what isn't. I mean, think about it…doesn't the Bible state that anyone who adds to or takes away from the Word is subject to some kind of judgment or punishment?"

Melena searched her memory bank of Bible verses. "I think so, but I'm not sure of the exact scripture, the context in which it was written, or the correct interpretation."

"Exactly," Pat said. "If it is the *complete, infallible* word of God then why are there so many interpretations? So many versions edited to include some pastor's opinion or point of view?"

Melena shook her head and shrugged. "I never pondered that."

Pat sighed. "I'm not trying to convert your way of thinking, Melena, just expand it, and to understand that scripture is open for interpretation by the reader, through the Holy Spirit, as it applies to his or her life at the time. Now don't get me wrong, I love the Word of God. I have several translations myself and I read them, study them—and then I ask questions and listen when He answers."

She took a deep breath and rolled her eyes heavenward. "Lord, help me stay on track with the issue at hand and not get on my proverbial soapbox."

Melena laughed.

Pat grinned. "I've been single for a long time, Mel, and trust me when I say, God and I have had some really deep conversations on the issue of sex. I love Him with every fiber of my being, but the truth is we are physical creatures with physical needs. *He* created us that way. Now, I'm not saying you, I, or *anyone* for that matter, should take a physical relationship lightly. As a nurse and an Energy

Medicine practitioner, I can honestly say one-night stands and frivolous, meaningless sex, though they may be the norm, are not healthy on any level–physical, emotional or spiritual.

"No one should share his or her most intimate self with another, if the heart is not attached and engaged. That said, I'll advise you like I do others...When a man and woman respect and care about each other, sex is a natural extension of the relationship. However, not every connection has to begin, or end, with marriage or even living together. There is a time and a season for every relationship we encounter.

"Some, like ours, are meant to last a lifetime, others aren't. Sex is something that should be talked about, prayed over, and *enjoyed*, not an impulse that brings shame or regret later down the road. For many that means marriage. Others insist on committed, exclusive, long term. My point is, the conditions of the relationship should be determined by the people involved and each person should take into consideration his or her, and their partner's, upbringing and beliefs *before* embarking on a physical relationship."

She smoothed her knuckles across Melena's flaming cheek. "You're my best friend and I love you more than anyone else in the world. I don't want to see you hurt or confused. Just be careful with these guys. With any man for that matter."

Melena shook her head. "I still can't believe we're even discussing this."

Pat laughed and gave her a hug. "As I said, someone's got to look after you."

"Why? Don't you think I'm capable of taking care of myself?"

Pat smiled. "Of course you are. But you're also refreshingly innocent, Mel, and that's a good thing. Just don't get so wrapped up in the newness or excitement of a possible relationship that you lose sight of yourself and what God has for you to do. Take some time to discover the depths of who *you* really are and can be. Don't let anyone dissuade you from that." She sighed. "Okay, enough preaching for one day."

Melena rolled her eyes. "Thank goodness."

They laughed and then headed out, determined to explore the surrounding towns.

Chapter Ten

Excitement warred with trepidation as Melena packed her suitcases. The ranch's busiest season had ended and now it was time for her to return to Mississippi. Pat's visit two weeks ago had ignited a firestorm of emotions until Melena thought she'd go mad. Desires long denied and buried exploded into passion so fierce she could hardly think or focus on anything but the needs of her body. She'd done everything in her power to resist the lures of her flesh and honestly felt as though she'd lose her grip. Dreams fueled the fires and had her nerves on edge so much that she'd snapped one night while out dancing with the crew.

What started out as laughter and teasing with Garrett and Kidd nearly turned into a confrontation when she stormed out of the club. Shelley followed.

"What in the hell's going on?"

Melena massaged her throbbing temples. "Those two are about to drive me nuts!"

"They seem to be laying on the charm pretty thick."

"Yeah, like some teenage competition on who will bed the little widow first."

"Whoa," Garrett interrupted.

Neither had heard him walk up.

Kidd sidled into view. "We're just joking, Melena, as always. Didn't mean to make you uncomfortable."

The sorrow and concern on their faces showed Melena that her own turmoil hadn't allowed her to process their banter as easily as she'd done in the past. "Apology accepted. Guess it's just me. I'm ready to go home."

They'd left the club, quiet and subdued.

This morning she'd awakened from one of the sweetest dreams she'd had in a long time, the content of which still had her reeling.

Her frustration and longing dissipated, and in its place rested a sense of assurance and confidence that even if she wasn't, God *was* in complete control of her thoughts, feelings and emotions.

She clasped the wedding bands, which she'd taken to wearing on a chain around her neck and eyed her vacant ring finger. Emptiness throbbed like a sore tooth. An image flashed in her mind of a delicate rose ring Jon had given her right before his death. One she had never worn because the only place it fit was the spot her wedding ring had occupied for thirty years.

The symbolism was not lost on her as Melena dug the ring out of its box, understanding now why she'd carried it in her purse from the moment he'd given it to her. Closing her eyes, she slid the ring on her finger with a silent vow. *I am Yours now, Lord, and You are mine. When I love again, I will be ready. I will be whole. And nobody, no other person's views or opinions, can take that choice from me. Help me stay true to myself, to You, and to the plan and purpose You have for me now.*

A knock on the door interrupted her musings.

"It's open, come on in!"

Kidd removed his hat as he stepped through the entrance. He eyed the suitcases stacked by the door. "I sure wish you'd wait and leave tomorrow. It's so late to start out today."

Touched by his concern, Melena smiled. "I know, but I'm ready to get the drive underway. I promise to stay in touch though, and to stop when I get tired."

He sighed. "Okay, then. I'll help load your car." He tucked her overnight bag under his arm and picked up a suitcase in each hand. "Is this everything?"

Melena nodded. "I've already put my artwork and computer in the back seat. Those go in the trunk. I'll double check while you carry them out."

She made another search through the rooms and was ready to leave when he stepped back through the entrance and closed the door behind him.

"Got it all?"

"Yes."

The gentleness of his touch belied the roughness of his calloused hands when he reached out and pulled her close. "May I kiss you goodbye?"

Her breath hitched. "Oh, Kidd...I..."

Hope and expectation collided with fear in his gaze and halted her protests.

She cocked an eyebrow. "Do you kiss and tell, cowboy?"

"Never," he vowed and took her face in his hands. His lips covered hers in a caress so tender she whimpered. Melena lost herself in the exquisite emotions swirling through her senses. *Sweet.*

Kidd must have felt the lack of sparks too. He ended the kiss, grinned and stepped back, his eyes lit with humor. "Will you be back soon?"

"Not to work, but I'm sure I'll be back at least a couple of weeks before the art show."

"Well, guess I'll see you in a couple of months."

Melena laid her palm against his cheek. "Take care of yourself and don't give up on your lady friend."

He sighed, covered her hand with his, moved it around to his mouth, and kissed the palm. "You take care also and call me anytime, day or night, if you need to talk."

"Thank you." Melena pressed her lips to the spot where her hand had rested moments before. She stepped aside for him to open the door. They walked out on the porch just as Garrett strolled up to the steps. His eyes narrowed, jaw muscle twitched.

"Heard you were leaving. Thought I'd see if you needed any help packing or loading your car."

Melena's heart thudded at the flare in his eyes and the edge to his voice. "That's sweet, but I'm all packed and loaded."

She turned to Kidd. "Thanks again for your assistance. Tell everyone I'll be down in a minute to see them before I leave."

Kidd's gaze cut to Garrett, but he left to do as she asked.

Garrett stepped closer. "Hoped you wouldn't leave without saying goodbye."

"Of course I wouldn't."

He reached around her and pushed open the door from which she'd just exited. "Sure you've got everything?"

She nodded. "Already checked."

"Check again," he urged and pulled her into the living room.

Before she could react or protest, he had her backed up against the wall, her body pressed firm against his chest, and his arms wrapped around her so tight she could scarcely breathe. Where Kidd's kiss was tender, gentle, Garrett's was anything but. His lips swooped over hers in an embrace that robbed her of the very air she needed to live. A kiss so fierce her knees threatened to buckle. Sensations battered her like a thousand tiny tornadoes until she found herself plastered against him, her hands fisted in his hair, her mouth demanding as much as his.

A guttural sound echoed in his throat and Garrett hauled her closer still for a brief, desperate moment, then eased her away.

"I'm not going to finish this here and now, not like this," he said, his voice raw, eyes fierce. "You're much too precious for that. But you think about it all those nights while you're home, alone, and hurry back." His eyes softened, tone gentled. "I've got a ride scheduled in less than fifteen minutes, so I won't be in the lodge when you stop by. Take care of yourself. Call anytime you want to talk. Come back soon." He brushed his lips across hers in a tender caress, opened the door and walked out.

Melena crumpled onto the nearest chair. Her breath escaped in jagged pants. *Sparks indeed!* Tiny pinpoints of pleasure bathed her senses in light and color. Electrical vibrations skittered and jumped along every nerve she possessed. She placed a hand against her body lest the pounding organ in her chest should hammer its way out. A sob shuddered through her. She pressed a fist against her lips and willed some semblance of control to her racing pulse.

She had no clue whether a moment or an eternity passed before she rose and walked into the kitchenette on rickety legs. She splashed cold water on her face and reached for a paper towel, then dried her cheeks. How she managed to get through the other goodbyes without blubbering like an idiot, she would never know.

The one-mile drive to the gate felt like a thousand. Melena passed Garrett and his guests on the trail, saw his wave in the rearview mirror, and felt his eyes on her long after she left the ranch. The hours and miles flew by in a mixture of sorrow and jubilation. Phone calls from her family and Pat kept her energized and awake despite the late departure from Utopia. Calls from her friends at the ranch made her ache to turn around and go back.

When night closed in around her and fatigue began to numb her mind and affect her reflexes, Melena pulled into a hotel and checked in. The next morning, she moseyed through her morning routine of coffee, reading and journaling and then checked her email, surprised to find one from Missy urging her to stop and visit when she passed through Louisiana. Melena emailed her back with a promise to do so. Hours later, she turned into the parking lot of the Visitor's Bureau, glad to find it empty except for one lone vehicle.

Melena climbed from her car and hurried in, anxious to see her young friend and catch up before continuing her trip home.

A long while after she left Missy, she pulled into her driveway and barely had time to relish the sigh of relief when the door flung open and her entire family flew from the house with shouts of joy at her return.

The evening passed in a blaze of activity as the welcome home party escalated to feverish pitch then fizzled. By the time the last guest left, and Melena righted her house, exhaustion took precedence and sleep claimed her mind and cocooned her body in peace and safety.

*****

Garrett Saunders propped his arms behind him, rested his head in clasped hands, and crossed long, denim-clad legs at the ankle. Though necessary to accommodate his large frame, the king-sized bed tended to be lonely. Especially when his thoughts were so full of a woman, his dreams fueled by a passion he had never known nor believed existed.

Not just any woman.

The thought curled through him like a caress.

For a moment, he allowed the sweetness to carry him away. Much like that first sip of rare, vintage wine. He chuckled softly and wondered if any true cowboy knew about vintage wine. Just one of the many secrets he kept close to his vest.

No one knew of the shame and abuse he'd suffered, abandoned as a child, or the fortune he'd made as an adult, and the agony that had ended life as he knew it. And, if he had his druthers, it would stay that way.

Garrett knew the past had a way of catching up with a person. No need to run too far or too fast, but hopefully, it would be a while before it caught up with him again. The memories and the pain were all buried once more, this time beneath blue jeans and boots.

He'd spent twenty years escaping his reality, his identity changing as often as his location. He'd backpacked through Europe, hidden in the jungles of Africa, the forests of Asia, and the mountains of Switzerland. He'd traipsed the United States, Central and South America, and knew Canada like the back of his hand. But he hadn't found true peace until he set foot on the Crossed Penn Ranch in Utopia, Texas.

And met the pretty widow from Mississippi.

One look at Melena Rhyker and his world, which had tilted on its axis years ago, righted itself, and he knew his running had ceased.

Unless of course he had to run after her. Which, he admitted to himself, wouldn't be a bad thing.

A shadow crossed his window. Garrett sat up, immediately on guard, his senses fine-tuned to the slightest change in atmosphere. Reaching for the pistol he kept in the bedside table drawer, he checked the clip then snapped it into place. Displaying the stealth with which he'd been raised and trained to operate, he slid from the bed and walked to the window. Quiet, careful, and with as little movement as he could marshal, he slipped the curtain away from the wooden frame, and lifted a slat on the blind. A huge buck reached up to nibble leaves off a tree not fifty yards away. Relief shivered through Garrett. He allowed the beauty and majesty of the moment to pervade his senses. Just as quietly as before, he moved to the bed, put the gun away, grabbed his camera and went to work.

Two hours and nearly a hundred photos later, he sat at the computer cropping, editing and rearranging as the idea for his next creation came to life. The phone rang, breaking his concentration.

"Yes?"

A pause, then, "Garrett?"

Like the song of a siren, her voice pulled him all the way out of the world he saw through the lens of creativity. "Hey, pretty lady."

"Did I catch you at a bad time?"

"No. I was just…" He hesitated. His photography art was another secret he held close. "Working on a project."

"Oh, well, sorry I interrupted."

He heard the hesitation in her voice. "Hey, no problem. What's up?"

"Nothing, been on the phone all morning with friends from the ranch. Shelley told me it was your day off so I thought I'd call and see how you're doing."

This time he heard the tremble and the anguish. He pushed away from the desk and the computer screen. She needed his undivided attention. "Are you okay?"

She sniffled. "Just lonesome. I guess."

"So when are you coming back?"

"Still not sure. I've been going and doing and playing catch-up since I got home two weeks ago. Now that it's all done, I'm kinda lost."

"I didn't hear the word 'painting' or 'creating' in there."

"'Cause there hasn't been either. I can't seem to settle or focus enough."

"Then you need to get back to the ranch."

She emitted a tiny laugh and his gut twisted with need.

"That's what Anne said too."

"So why aren't you on your way already?"

"Because the anniversary of Jon's death is coming up and it's bound to be hard on the kids and grandkids. I need to stay. For their sake. I should be here for them."

"Says who?"

She stuttered, unable to form a reply.

"Give me Pat's number."

"Why?"

"I'm going to get her on your ass. Maybe then, you'll listen to reason. There is no law of morality or etiquette that says you have to stay where you're unhappy or unfulfilled regardless of whose sake you're doing it for. You're not the first or the only person who's suffered loss, born the weight of grief, or had to figure out how to put a shattered life back together and learn to live again and plan for the future."

She gasped. Silence, then a dial tone. Garrett hung up with a curse.

So much for keeping the past at bay.

He lunged from his chair so hard it nearly toppled. Paced the floor of the small log cabin he rented. Stalked back into the room he used as an office and shut down the project he'd started. No sense in trying to work when he was so riled up. A muttered curse escaped his clenched teeth. Why'd he have to fall boots over spurs for a newly widowed woman? Why not some uncomplicated female with no past?

Because no past usually means no substance, no essence. You need an equal partner, someone who can heal you, as you help her to heal.

The voice sprang out of nowhere, sent shivers along his spine.

He closed his eyes and rolled his head, then shoulders to ease the tension building there. This wasn't the first time he'd heard that voice, those words. *Who are you? What do you want?* He tamped down the questions burning within.

They echoed back. Taunting. *Who are* you *and what do* you *want?*

"I just want peace," he muttered.

Peace starts within and comes from facing and dealing with your past, not running from it.

"It sure doesn't come from hearing voices," he argued.

A chuckle sounded in his mind.

Nor talking with them, the voice replied.

As much as he tried to avoid direct contact on a regular basis, for their protection and his, Garrett knew the time soon approached when he'd have to get together with his ancestral tribe's shaman. He clenched his fists, gritted his teeth, and glared at the ceiling. "I don't want this."

You are chosen, gifted. What is there not to want?

The responsibility. Garrett sighed and dragged a hand through his hair. He didn't want the responsibility the gift carried. Which is why he'd run from it his entire life.

He picked up his phone, dialed Melena's number then let out a low growl when the call went straight to voicemail.

Chapter Eleven

Melena resisted the urge to hurl the phone. *Of all the unmitigated gall!* Before she could finish berating Garrett in her mind, much less speak the words aloud, her phone rang. His name flashed on caller ID. She declined the call. Minutes later, the phone jangled again. She ignored this call and the next. An hour after the third call, she checked her messages. Butterflies bounced off her ribcage when she listened to his voice...

"Melena, I know you've got this damn phone with you."

Little remorse here. She hit delete.

The next message heaved a sigh through the air. "Mel, don't make me apologize by voice mail."

"You don't know me well enough to call me Mel," she muttered. She hit delete again and waited for the next message.

A vile curse greeted her ear. "Fine, give me the silent treatment. I thought we were way past the games teenagers play."

Melena barely had time to process the tug of anger at his tone, followed by remorse because he was right, when a text message came through.

"All right, have it your way. I'm sorry. I was out of line. Please call so I can apologize in person."

Much better. She smiled and hit the redial button.

"Apology accepted," she interjected before he could say more than her name.

"I have no right to tell you how to grieve and I'm sorry I was short with you, but you need to do what's best for *you*. Everyone else should respect your feelings as much as you do theirs."

Truth rang with startling clarity in his words. Melena blinked fast, swallowed hard and sighed. "I know, but it's so difficult to know what the right thing to do is. I've always been here for my children and now, with the grandkids..."

Her voice trembled. She cleared her throat. "I mentioned going back to the ranch and my mother thinks I'm just running away."

"So, what's wrong with running away, or more aptly, running *to* something? Your children will learn to respect you more if you stand up for what you believe is best for your healing. Besides, you can always go back."

"That's a long trip for a short visit."

This time it was Garrett's turn to sigh. "You're right. Well, get back as soon as you feel comfortable, and call anytime. I promise I won't bite your head off next time."

She heard the smile in his voice and envisioned the dimple in his cheek and those deep, azure eyes sparkling with mirth. Her lips curved in response. "Thank you."

They chatted a little longer, then hung up.

Melena put the phone in her pocket and pressed a hand against the thundering in her chest. She turned and caught a glimpse of Jon smiling at her from her favorite photograph. Everything within her spiraled as the voice of guilt rose to taunt.

Hasn't even been a year yet...

She grabbed the picture and sank onto her bed. Fresh sobs wracked her frame until she fell into an exhausted slumber and dreamt...

They danced. Jon held her close as they glided across the floor. They whirled and twirled to the strains of a waltz.

"I love you," she whispered.

His entire being lit up. "I love you too, Mel. But you have to let me go."

His words tore at her. "I don't want to...I miss you so much."

The pain intensified until she felt as though she were being split in two. "Please, Jon, don't leave me again."

The music waned. He drifted away. She clung and cried but couldn't hold on to him.

"Let me go," he repeated, and the words echoed in the space where he'd held her.

The phone rang and jolted her awake. Her pillow was soaked. She grabbed the receiver. "Hello."

Pat's voice came over the line. "What's going on, hon?"

"Just having a crazy, emotional day." A sob escaped. "Oh, Pat, I can't do this! I don't want to. I'm never going to get through this!"

"Yes, you will. Hang on. I'll be over in a bit."

Melena hung up the phone, rolled over, clasped Jon's pillow to her breast and sobbed. When the doorbell rang, she stumbled from the bed, opened it and fell into her friend's arms.

"Oh, honey, I wish I could take this pain from you. I wish I knew what to say."

"There's nothing anyone can say. He's gone, he's never coming back, and it hurts so much I can hardly breathe! Feels like a thousand tiny spears tearing at every fiber of my being."

Pat cradled Melena, stroked her hair, and rocked until the sobs subsided. "Want to talk or go somewhere?"

Melena shook her head.

"What can we do to help you feel better?"

"I just want to throw myself on his grave and rage until they haul me off in a straitjacket or I curl up and die."

"Well, that's not going to happen. If you want to go to the cemetery, we'll go, and you can lie down and cry until you're bone dry. But no one is hauling you off, nor will you curl up and die. I'll be there to help you back up on your feet and bring you home or wherever you want to go."

"I want to go back to the ranch."

"What's stopping you?"

"It's a long drive for a short trip and I need to be here for the anniversary."

"Says who?"

"Everyone! They think I'm just running away. No one understands that I can't run from this pain, it follows me everywhere! But there's so much peace at the ranch, such a healing energy. I seem to flourish there but nobody seems to care about that. They all think they know what's best for me! How can they know when I have no clue? All I know is that I don't feel whole or at peace here without Jon."

"Then you need to go there."

"But what about my family?"

Pat urged Melena to her feet. "Let's both go. We'll pack a bag, just enough for a few days, leave tonight and share the driving. If you honestly feel you have to be here on the anniversary, then we'll drive back. If not, we'll stay until you are ready to return."

"That's crazy. We'd be going just to turn around and come back. Besides, I have to be in Utopia before the art festival and my show anyway."

"You think staying here and crying yourself into exhaustion or a nervous breakdown is a better idea?"

"I don't know," Melena cried.

"Yes, you do," Pat insisted. "Listen to your inner voice, not your head. We can fly and rent a car or have someone from the ranch pick us up. There are so many options. You just need to open up to them."

Melena sighed. "Let's check the flights."

"That's my girl." Pat squeezed her hand and led Melena toward the room where her computer sat on the desk.

Within moments, they'd checked flight schedules and prices and decided driving was their best bet.

Melena packed a suitcase, art supplies and her laptop and within the hour, they were on their way. They arrived at the ranch in time for breakfast.

"You're back!" Marcey squealed and flung herself in Melena's arms when she walked through the lodge door. Alerted by the exuberant greeting, others came from various directions to embrace Melena and Pat. Enveloped in warmth, tears streamed down Melena's cheeks.

"I'm such a mess," she blubbered. "I just couldn't seem to focus or rest or even think!"

Anne enfolded her in a fierce hug then turned to Pat. "I'm so glad you brought her here."

Pat smiled. "Not sure how long we'll stay but she needed to get back here, if only for a day or two.”

“Well, we’ll get y’all settled in a room. Melena, you know where your studio is if you feel inspired. If not, just rest. We’ve plenty of art for the show.”

“We don’t mind staying in the bunkhouse,” Melena assured.

Marcey grinned. “Can’t, it’s being renovated for Kidd’s new wife and kids.”

Surprise widened Melena’s eyes. Barely a month ago, the man flirted with, teased and kissed *her*. “That was quick.”

Marcey chuckled and held out her hand. “Not really, we, well rather *I*, was just too stubborn to see what was right before my eyes.”

Melena’s jaw dropped. “Wow! Really?” She embraced Marcey again. “Congratulations!”

“It’s all your fault, you know,” Marcey teased.

Melena arched a brow. “Oh?”

“Yeah, all your talk about soul mates and figuring out what I really wanted opened my eyes to the truth of who he really is. We’ve always gotten along and had fun together, but I ignored the deeper feelings because I was so dead set against a cowboy, thinking most aren’t settled or responsible. I mean, I watched him flirt with every female who walked in the door and that just confirmed my fears that he was like the other men I’d met. *And married*. But then we sat down one night and had a really long conversation and I realized I’d judged him unfairly. He’d been telling me that from the beginning, but I was too stubborn to see it.” They turned as the door opened and Kidd walked through.

A flush filled Marcey’s cheeks, the unmistakable light of love brightened her eyes. Melena watched him walk up and noted how everything about them softened toward one another.

Kidd slid his arm around Melena's waist then bent to kiss her cheek. "Welcome back," he drawled.

Marcey giggled. "He still flirts with every woman that walks in."

Kidd grinned, moved close and skimmed his lips over Marcey's. "All part of the job, ma'am, and the charm which captured you."

He turned back to Melena. "I tried to get over her, to move on and stay open to the fact that God may have had another woman in mind. But deep down I knew she's the one for me. I just had to be patient and give her the room and freedom to make that discovery on her own."

"Really?" Melena asked with a pointed look.

"Could have fooled me," Pat interjected. "I'd have sworn you didn't have an ounce of permanency in you."

Kidd chuckled. "All part of the plan to keep myself open and let this one know what she was missing." He winked at Marcey. "I have been sorely tempted by a bevy of women to walk away and forget her, even tried a time or two. Somehow though, when the dust settled and the others left, my feelings remained steadfast."

Melena sighed and embraced them. "I'm so happy for both of you," she said, while her entire being cried out against what was missing in her own life. She sniffled and gazed around. "Garrett's off again today?"

"Yep. Left yesterday. Some unexpected business or something. Didn't explain much, say where he was going, or for how long." Kidd carried her and Pat's suitcases up to the room Anne assigned. He turned and touched Melena's cheek.

"It is really good to see you. You look tired."

"I am," Melena admitted.

"Well, get some rest. Y'all want us to hold breakfast a bit for you?"

"Not me," she and Pat answered in unison.

Kidd tipped his hat then backed out of the room. "See you ladies at lunch then."

Melena flopped down on a bed as every ounce of tension she'd felt over the last few days escaped in a sigh. "Oh, it is so good to be here."

Pat kicked off her shoes and climbed into the other bed. "Sure is. So, are you going to tell me about that look you and Kidd shared and why you're so glum that Garrett's not here?"

"Nothing to the look but surprise, and I'm not glum, just disappointed. I'd hoped to see everyone before we leave again."

Pat snorted and arched an eyebrow at her. "Tell that to someone who doesn't know you so well."

Melena ached to tell her best friend how she felt, but guilt congealed the words in her throat. "Just tired," she mumbled, then curled into a fetal position facing away from Pat.

* * * * *

Pat listened to Melena's unsteady breathing and ached at the pain her friend was experiencing. She took several deep breaths and allowed her mind to empty. Slow warmth spread through her as she slipped into a deep, meditative state.

"Open my eyes that I may see," she whispered and felt the shift as her spiritual eye responded. "My ears that I may hear, my mind that I may understand, and my heart that I may receive." Each part of her spirit awakened and tuned in to her Divine Master. She sensed Him first and then saw the Lord Jesus, arms wide open to embrace her. Pat felt the warmth and strength of His love and compassion as she reached out for wisdom and grace. *Help me to help her.*

Emotions bombarded her...fear, anxiety, sadness, guilt. Pain gripped her soul. Jon appeared and, like a film reel or mini movie, images of his and Melena's life flashed in her mind's eye.

"Teach her."

The edict echoed and shuddered through her entire being and Pat knew Melena's life purpose was just beginning.

Chapter Twelve

Garrett reclined with his grandfather, the Chief, and the Shaman of his Native American tribe. He hadn't participated in the religious rituals of his tribe in years but had often enjoyed the camaraderie of sitting with them in the lodge. Today, though, Garrett knew he was in for the whole experience. Sweat poured from his brow, toxins flowed from his pores.

Where his ancestors had used drums and sang songs to the Creator, a small CD player and concealed speakers provided those now. That didn't stop the elders from joining in with the chants and prayers. His grandfather lit the sacred pipe, took a drag, and passed it around. Garrett didn't have to use the pipe to inhale the herbs and spices burning in its bowl. He pulled in a deep breath, braced himself for the visions to come. And they would, had for years, in sacred places all over the world, and in parts unknown to most common people. Sometimes welcomed, sometimes hated, he still had trouble reconciling this part of his heritage and these experiences with his understanding of Christian values and deep love for Christ.

Like an eagle soaring high above the earth, his spirit flew. Images of what transpired below appeared. He saw Melena lying across a grave. Sobs shook her small frame. Pain stabbed through him, congealed in his chest. The eagle landed in a nearby tree.

Garrett waited, anxious, alert. A man appeared below the tree and gazed up at him.

"She's special."

Garrett acknowledged the comment with a nod.

"She needs someone strong, someone open and flexible."

Garrett allowed the man's aura to expand until it touched his and braced himself for the onslaught of emotions that would follow. Profound love. Acute sorrow. Pain lanced through him until he couldn't catch his breath. He struggled against it then surrendered.

Light—golden, brilliant, glowing—enveloped him in its warmth. Angels accompanied by his spirit guide (another embodiment of his Native American heritage) embraced him, then turned and bent their knees as Jesus approached.

Garrett bowed in reverence. "My Lord."

The Lord capped a hand over his head and Garrett's mind filled.

"The Archangel Michael accompanies you. Call on him in your times of duress and he shall guide your steps."

He jerked to awareness. The rocks hissed as someone stoked the fire beneath and trickled water onto their heated surface. He sat up, scrubbed the heels of his hands over his face, then rose. His grandfather and the Shaman rose with him. Garrett embraced each of them, then strode out of the wigwam into the bright Arizona sunlight. He would spend another night here with the tribe then return to Texas on the morrow.

He awoke the next morning before dawn and was on the road within minutes. As it had coming up, the return trip would take the better part of twenty-four hours. A thermos of coffee lay next to a small chest filled with ice, drinks and snacks. Cheese, fruit, nuts, and water—filtered and bottled in handmade pottery jars crafted by his people. He'd always been conscious of what went into his body. With the exception of coffee, his one weakness, and an occasional night on the town which included alcoholic beverages, he managed to stay healthy and fit.

As the distance piled up behind him, his eyes and reflexes remained alert and firmly in the present, while Garrett's mind wandered through the journey of his past. Memories rolled in and through, quick flashes of image followed by the sharp edge of anger, the wrench of sadness, or tug of regret. A little boy abused and frightened, the young man, angry and defiant. His years of running, not in fear, but out of a desperate need to protect those he loved. His passion for photography, the places he traveled and the success that talent brought him.

Stopping when needed and only for as long as necessary, the miles flew by with him barely aware of the change of scenery. From the rich, desert landscape to deep mountainous terrain, the vast emptiness of the west Texas plains to the intimate coziness of the Hill Country. He arrived at his cabin eighteen hours after leaving Arizona.

Garrett stumbled from the truck, fumbled his way into the house and tumbled into bed fully clothed. Fueled by exhaustion, dreams wound their way through his subconscious until he awoke four hours later, chest pounding, breathing labored and skin slick and clammy with sweat. He lunged from the bed, stripped as he went, and stood a long time in the shower. His stomach gnawed on his backbone a bit, then grumbled noisily. Donning pajama pants and a t-shirt, he padded into the kitchen just as dawn broke over the horizon in a glorious display of light and color.

Garrett opened the window, took a deep breath of the fresh,

morning air, and felt his whole body relax. He prepared a bowl of cereal, carried it into the living room and kicked back in his recliner to eat. He awoke two hours later, this time refreshed.

She's here.

The thought reverberated through his entire being even before the text from Kidd came through telling him Melena was at the ranch.

Be there in a bit, he typed, then sent the message off. He spent the next few minutes exchanging correspondence with Kidd and learned when Melena and Pat had arrived, then dressed and headed out to the Crossed Penn.

Garrett felt a shift in his emotions the moment he drove through the ranch gate. Everything within him lifted. As though his spirit stood up and danced. Visions of twirling light filled his senses until the air around him hummed. He stopped his truck and went into the lodge through the front entrance, where Pat sat alone, shredding a napkin.

She glanced up.

Their eyes met. Souls touched. Minds connected.

He tipped his hat then removed it as he pulled out a chair to join her. "How is she?"

Pat's eyes revealed the depth of her concern. She shook her head.

"Not doing too well. She's so...lost, broken, and I don't know how to help her."

"Your just being here helps her."

Pat's hand shook as she reached for her coffee while the other continued to knead the remains of the napkin. "Yeah, I'd like to believe that. I never realized how close they were. How painful this is for her. How inept I'd be at helping the one person I love most in my life."

Garrett placed a hand over hers and stilled the restless movements. "You are far from inept, better for her than you realize."

Pat sipped, put the cup down and locked eyes with him, saw everything he felt, and smiled. "You'll be good for her too. You won't stem her growth or hold her back. Not that Jon did. He just didn't understand the depths she is capable of. You do. You two are cut from the same cloth."

She shook her head when Garrett shifted in his chair. "Don't pull back or deny. Don't run this time."

His gaze narrowed, sharpened. "You know."

She nodded. "A lot more than you think."

A movement above drew their attention. Both glanced up as Melena started down the stairs. She hesitated, then a smile bloomed. "Garrett!"

She hurried down the stairs and into his embrace as he stood.

"Hey, pretty lady."

"I didn't think we'd see you this time. Kidd said he thought you had an emergency or something. Everything okay?"

"Much better now." He pulled a chair out for her.

"Thanks, I need a cup of coffee before I sit though."

"I'll get it," Pat said and rose to do so.

"So, how long are you gonna be here?" Garrett asked.

Melena's sigh spoke volumes. "Not sure. The anniversary of Jon's death is next week, and the art show less than two weeks after that. Anne says we have enough work but...I don't know. Something keeps pulling at me. Though I have no clue what it is or will be. Thought I'd take a hike after while and see what comes to mind."

"Still undecided whether or not you should be home for the anniversary?"

She nodded, sipped coffee and tried to explain the paradox of emotions at war within. "I'm so torn. My heart tells me one thing, my mind another."

"What does your soul say?"

Melena closed her eyes, took a deep breath and tried to connect with that still, small voice within. "My soul seems to only be at peace, to be settled, here."

"Then this is where you should stay."

"But no one seems to understand that except you two. Even I don't understand. It's all so confusing! I'm constantly overwhelmed with indecision."

Pat reached over and gave Melena a hug. "That's why it's important to listen to your soul. The deepest part of your being. Other people may think they know what's best for us, but that's usually based on what they feel, what they need. The human mind is not always a reliable source, as it is crowded with chatter from years of upbringing, other folks' opinions, what we've heard, read, or been taught. Our emotions are in the habit of going off on a tangent by themselves, based on what we think or feel. That, in itself, can be disastrous. But the soul, the very core of our being, knows what is best for us, whether or not it makes sense to our rational mind.

"I just want to do what's right."

"By whose standards?" Garrett asked.

Melena shrugged.

He snorted. "And therein lies the problem. At some point in our lives, in our spiritual journey, we have to set our own standards. Not based on what 'they'"—he finger-quoted the word—"think."

"But *how* do I do that?"

"Get quiet, centered, and ask—God, Jesus, Holy Spirit, your angels and/or spirit guides—whatever term or terms you use to connect with your Divine Source, for guidance. Then listen to what you're told. Don't argue or second guess. Just listen. And obey."

"I just wish I knew what Jon thought. What he'd want me to do."

"Then ask *him*."

Melena's head jerked up, eyes clouded. "What?"

Pat narrowed her gaze at Garrett in warning and took Melena's hand in hers. "Mel, Jon's spirit lives on and is with you at all times. You can ask him for guidance and direction too. The problem with that might be disbelieving and discerning what you actually hear, from what you know or feel he would say because of your years together."

"I don't understand."

"Jon is in a place of pure love so whatever guidance he gives you will come from that aspect. Not the physical plane where thoughts and emotions rule." She patted Melena's shoulder. "Enough of all this for now. Do you want to eat before your hike?"

Melena got up, poured another cup of coffee and grabbed a couple of cookies. She glanced at the clock then shook her head and bit into the soft, decadent dough. "This'll do for now. Lunch is less than an hour away. I'll wait."

She carried the snack up to her room, finished it, brushed her teeth, grabbed her camera and headed out. Her mind whirled with everything that had been said, but Melena shoved it all aside and simply absorbed the serenity around her.

Meanwhile, back in the lodge, Pat glared at Garrett. "You can't teach her spiritual truth by shoving it down her throat all at once."

Garrett rose, slapped his hat on his head and scowled. "Small doses might be easier to digest but sometimes they're not as effective. Especially when you sugar coat them."

He turned on his heel and strode out through the kitchen, leaving Pat to ponder if her methods of helping Melena were unduly influenced by emotion.

* * * * *

Melena walked up the hill behind the lodge, away from buildings and people, and tried to keep her mind clear, heart and spirit open, but found she wasn't really in a creative mood. If something caught her eye, she snapped a picture but didn't put much effort into angles, distance and focus, or shadows and contrast. She continued her journey and let everything go. All thoughts, every emotion drained away as she absorbed the serene atmosphere around her. The trail she took led to a bench on top of a hill, overlooking a glorious profusion of trees, rock and sky.

"I need some guidance here." She whispered the words, not wanting to break the stillness, the peace, she felt while hiking. Then she sat, determined to be quiet and to hear what her soul wanted to say.

This is what I need. The serenity, the beauty and tranquility of these hills. Everything about this place calms my spirit, stirs my creativity.

And therein lay her answer.

The moment Melena realized that, her mind jumped into the conversation, arguing, accusing, and laying on the guilt. She covered her ears, bent her head and took several deep breaths. "Peace, be still," she whispered, and repeated the phrase until the indignant chatter in her brain calmed once again.

She sat a while longer, walked some more and prayed for the courage to do what she knew had to be done.

Arriving back at the lodge, she went into the office and called her son.

"Hey, Mom, everything okay?"

"I'm good, Jon. Much better now that I'm here. So much so, that I'm not coming home until after the art show."

"What?"

She recoiled at the shock in his voice, but Melena stood her ground. "I just can't be there."

"But I thought we'd take the day off, spend it together, be there for each other."

"And that's a lovely thought, honey. But I just can't. I know it's hard to grasp this. Believe me, it's difficult to explain. But I can't stand the agony of being in that house, or even that town without your father. You have no idea how many times I thought about how easy it would be to end this pain."

"Don't even say that, Mom!"

"I'm not threatening, Jon. Just trying to tell you how I feel. I would never do that to you kids, my parents, or my grandchildren. But the thought has been there, especially in those moments of sheer agony missing your father. I know grandma thinks I'm running away, but that's not it at all. Something about this place soothes my soul, gives me room to breathe, to grieve, and to heal. I can't find that at home. I don't know why, but I just can't."

"You don't think seeing a counselor or joining a support group would help?"

"It might. But you see, I don't feel the need to do that here. Here, all I need is to *be*, to *feel*, and to process all of these emotions. My entire life, I've put others' feelings before mine. This time I need someone to appreciate my feelings, to see my point. Which is why I called you. You are the most compassionate, understanding man I know. So much like your father in your practicality, and yet, more like me in heart. Of all those I love, besides Pat, you are the one I trust most to comprehend my sentiments here. I *have* to do this. My peace of mind, my *sanity*, depends on it. I love you, Jon. I love you *all* and I hope everyone will come up for the art show, but if not, I'll see y'all after."

Seconds ticked by. Tension oozed over the line. Jon's sigh spoke volumes. "Okay, Mom. I get it. Not sure how everyone else will feel, but I'll do my best to help them understand where you're coming from. Do what you have to do for your highest good, your ultimate healing."

The breath she hadn't realized she was holding escaped Melena in a rush. "Thank you, Jon. I love y'all and I'll see you soon."

Chapter Thirteen

Garrett ground his teeth. "I don't want to do this yet."

Anne's smile thinned; impatience simmered. "Then why did you come this time? We've handled your career from the beginning, invited you *and* featured your work every year since we opened this place. So why now?"

Garrett shrugged. "Just thought it'd be nice to stop for a while."

Anne Penn, his cousin and the only remaining relative on his mother's side, curled her lip and narrowed her eyes. "It's time for you to come out of the closet, let people know who you are and stop hiding behind all those aliases. Your stint with the CIA is over. Has been for years."

"I know that, which is why I'm using my real name now. Well, most of it anyway. Besides they were necessary while I was with the CIA."

She sat back, shook her head. "I don't understand why you're so reluctant, Garrett. What's done is done. The past is long since over with. He's dead and you've nothing to fear anymore."

Garrett lunged to his feet and smashed the hat onto his head. "I'm not afraid. I just don't want to relive the nightmare by 'coming out of the closet' as you so delicately put it."

She rose, reached a hand to his shoulder, rubbed to soothe. "I'm sorry. I don't mean to push but I feel deep in my spirit the time has come for your reveal party. The public has been crying for one for years."

Garrett removed her hand, lifted it to his mouth, kissed the back.

"And I can't thank you enough for that or for not pushing me before now. I'll think about it and let you know in a couple of days. Well, in time for the show," he promised before she could ask.

She knew when to stop pushing, he'd hand her that much. Garrett went out to the corral.

* * * * *

Melena walked down from the studio where she'd spent the better part of the afternoon. Though she hadn't worked on anything new, she'd spent hours arranging and rearranging her portraits, paintings and glass art, willing the restlessness to ease. It had, and now she wanted to mix and mingle with her friends and the few guests staying at the ranch. Passing by an open door, she peeked into another studio where Anne, a frown creasing her brow, muttered to herself while she moved stuff around. Melena knocked on the frame.

"Everything okay?"

Anne looked up from her chore, smiled and waved her in. "Yeah. How about you?"

"I'm good." She stopped. Her jaw dropped open at the display of photography art strewn about the room.

"Oh my, this is fabulous! Did you and/or Bill do this?"

Anne shook her head. "No, this is one of our regular featured artist's work. Look closely and you'll see his signature."

Melena walked as close as she dared to the stunning display and peered at the initials GS inscribed in a tiny white cloud in the bottom right corner of the framed collage. She frowned over at Anne. "GS? No, wait...I've heard of this artist, seen his work before...." Her eyes widened in awe. "GS Whitecloud. You know GS Whitecloud?"

Anne chuckled. "Known him all of my life—and his."

Melena dropped down onto a stool. "Seriously? Pray tell."

"He's a cousin on both mothers' side of our respective families."

"Guards his privacy very well from what I've heard and read," Melena remarked.

The frown returned between Anne's eyes. "I know. Been after him for a while to agree to a reveal party but he's pretty stubborn. Maybe this year though."

Melena's senses hummed. The hair on her arms and the back of her neck stood on end. "He's here, isn't he?"

Anne's shrug and noncommittal grunt didn't convince her. Melena walked around the room, examined. Wildlife and flowers, mountains and lakes, cities and country scenes all merged to create a masterpiece in each individual collage. Bits and pieces of his sketchy biography flitted through her brain.... *Native American descent, world traveler, talented, and gifted with a unique view of the planet and its inhabitants....*

"GS... Garrett Saunders," she deduced, then looked at the collages in a completely new light. "Garrett is GS Whitecloud?"

"I didn't say that," Anne hedged.

Melena laughed. "You haven't refuted it either."

Anne eyed her. "How'd you guess? He hasn't let anyone see him work or bring anything here. We've gone to great lengths to protect his identity and privacy."

Melena shrugged. "I just felt it was him. Besides, he's always got a camera with him. He pretends it's only to take pictures with or for guests, but it's always there. On hikes or trail rides, even the hayride."

"You're very intuitive. Most artists are. One can usually spot another."

"I never would have guessed before today and seeing this. He makes a real good cowboy." Melena's cheeks grew warm at the admission. "Don't worry, though, I'll do my best to respect his privacy and not betray your confidence."

Anne considered her for a moment before a smile bloomed and lit her entire face. "Don't do that."

Melena frowned. "What?"

"Confront him. Challenge him. He needs to be 'encouraged,'" Anne finger-quoted the word, "to agree to the reveal party. It'll boost his career to new heights. You don't have to make a point to do so, but if the topic of your show comes up or something, let him know that you know who he is."

"You sure?"

Anne nodded. A grin curved her lips. "Yeah, you just might be the perfect one to convince him."

"Convince who of what?"

Both women turned at the question.

Bill entered the room, a wary expression on his face. "What are you two conspiring about?"

Anne threw back her head and laughed while blood scorched Melena's cheeks.

Anne slipped one arm through Melena's, the other through her husband's. "Not conspiring, darling, collaborating. We're out to convince Garrett it's time to let the world know who he is."

"Sounds like a conspiracy to me." This time all three turned toward the door.

Garrett stepped through, his eyes narrowed at Anne. "I told you I'd give you an answer in a couple of days. You didn't have to involve her."

"She didn't involve me. I figured it out on my own." Melena jumped to Anne's defense. Those azure eyes sharpened, homed in on her and Melena sensed secrets far deeper and darker than artistic temperament lurking beneath the surface of his tightly controlled features.

"Maybe you should keep your pretty nose out of other folks' business." He turned on his heel and stormed out.

The air in the room vibrated in his wake.

Melena massaged the chill from her skin and willed her chattering pulse to calm. "Well, that went over about as smooth as shards of glass in a milkshake."

* * * * *

Garrett couldn't get away from the lodge fast enough. He strode to the corral, tightened the cinch of his saddle and mounted his horse. He shot out of the enclosed area and, within moments, had the stout gelding bounding over rocks and up the hill behind the ranch house. Reaching the top, he slowed the horse's pace until he stood alongside the bench overlooking most of the ranch.

Dismounting, Garrett looped his reins over the bench back and walked to the edge of the bluff. A squawk above got his attention and he watched as a hawk circled, cried out and dove into the brush then came back up with a small animal in his talons. That's what he felt like.... a tiny rodent trapped in the claws of something he couldn't fight, couldn't win against.

"What's there to fight, to win against?"

The voice came out of nowhere. Unbidden. Unwelcome.

"This trap," Garrett said, fist raised to the sky. "This never-ending nightmare and now these expectations. I just want peace and freedom."

"True peace, true freedom comes from acceptance and surrender. You've lived a lifetime circling around but avoiding both."

Garrett sat on the edge of the crag, allowed the anger and frustration to flow out with each breath and opened up. "How do I change that after all these years?"

The voice became that of his grandfather. "Listen to your guidance. Be true to yourself. Live with honesty, integrity and transparency. Your cousin is correct. There is nothing left to fear."

"Then why am I so afraid?"

"Deciding to live authentically after so many years of hiding behind who you are, or were, in the world's eyes can be intimidating."

Another voice, one he loved and revered even more than his grandfather's chimed in… "I have not given you a spirit of fear, but of love and power and a sound mind."

Garrett sat there until the swirl of emotions settled and flowed out, leaving peace in their wake. In that moment, he felt her. Melena had been in a similar quandary in this very spot earlier.

* * * * *

Gathered in Melena's studio, she, Pat and Anne discussed the upcoming show. Garrett hesitated, then knocked on the open door. Melena broke away from the other women and walked toward him.

"Garrett...."

He shook his head before she could say another word. "I want to apologize." His eyes swept the room, merged with Anne's. "To both of you."

Anne's acceptance of his words of contrition was a brief nod and brilliant smile. "I know I shouldn't push you so, but I really believe it's time to do this, Garrett."

Garrett removed his hat, fumbled with it then raked his fingers through his hair and mumbled, "Okay." He hesitated then narrowed his gaze at his cousin. "I'm going to say this one time and one time only. If things don't turn out the way you think they should and it all blows up in your face, don't come crying to me and *don't* say I didn't warn you."

"Agreed," Anne said with a nod of acquiescence.

Garrett turned and strode from the room.

Melena stroked the chill from her arms and took a deep breath. "He's got so much anger inside."

"Goes deeper than anger, I'd say," Pat chimed in.

"You're both right. He'll have to be the one to tell you more than that," Anne added, and staunchly warded off the questions burning in their gazes.

* * * * *

Get to the ranch, quick!

Garrett lunged from his bed and prayed as the words reverberated through the cabin. He dressed and headed out. Memories of his visions while in Arizona crowded his mind and, although he had no idea what was going on, he called on the Archangel Michael to intervene. The three miles from his place to the Crossed Penn seemed like a thousand and he sighed in relief as he drove up to the gate and punched in the security code. A movement by the pond snagged his attention. He glanced over as Melena, dressed in a flowing white gown, rushed toward the water.

He barreled through the gate, heard the scrape of iron against metal. Punching the accelerator, he bounced over the rocky terrain and bolted from the vehicle as she went in and under the murky water.

"Melena!" His shout echoed in the stillness of the night air as he plunged in after her.

She emerged, shaken and crying and he managed to grab her before she went under a second time.

"What are you doing?"

She gazed up at him, glassy-eyed. "I'm looking for Jon."

He shook her. "What?"

"Jon. Have you seen him?"

Assured she was either sleepwalking or hallucinating, Garrett folded her in his embrace, careful to be gentle. "He's not here, Melena. Let's get you out of this water before you catch your death."

She struggled as he led her from the pond. "But he told me to meet him here. What are you doing? Let me go!"

He yanked her up hard. "Melena, stop! Wake up now."

She went still in his grasp. Her eyes widened. Her vision sharpened. "Garrett? What happened? Where am I?"

He pulled the blanket he carried out from behind the seat of his truck and wrapped it around her. "You're sleepwalking. Went into the pond."

"Sleepwalking? I don't sleepwalk."

"Hallucinating then. Have you eaten anything strange or taken any drugs, prescription or otherwise?"

"No."

He helped her into the passenger seat of his truck and buckled her in. "You've never sleepwalked in your life? Never woke up in a different room or on the couch not knowing, not remembering how you got there?"

Melena frowned. "Maybe, as a child. I don't really know. Have to ask mom or dad. My daughter did a time or two when she was very young, but only because she was really stressed or overly tired. The only place I've woken up not knowing how I got there was on the floor by my bed."

"When did that start?"

"After Jon's death, but not for several months now, and certainly not here. Where are you taking me?" she asked when he turned his truck away from the lodge.

"My place. We both need to get dry and warm and I'll mix you up a batch of herbs to make into a tea that will help with these."

"Herbal teas, really?"

"There's a lot you don't know about me."

Melena nodded. "That's true enough. So much so, that I think you should just take me back to the lodge. I can take a warm shower and put on clean clothes myself."

"I doubt you thought to grab your room key in your sleep, do you really want to wake Pat or anyone else?"

Melena sighed at the dilemma and wrapped the blanket a bit tighter around her shoulders. "I guess not."

"I promise not to take advantage of you nor let you take advantage of me," Garrett said with a chuckle.

Chapter Fourteen

Within a few minutes, they were ensconced in Garrett's cabin. He showed Melena the bathroom and insisted she shower first. He then went into his bedroom, where he unlocked and lifted the lid of a tiny trunk he hadn't ventured to open in more than a quarter century. Unprepared for the sharp stab of grief and rage, he sat on the floor and pulled out the beaded tunic dress, leggings, and moccasins that once belonged to his sister. She'd been ten years younger than Garret, and the two had been reared in entirely different surroundings. Her death at the hands of their father when she was sixteen had changed Garrett's life forever.

He felt a movement behind him, then Melena's hand on his shoulder.

"Garrett?"

He turned to find her wrapped in his robe.

"I called for you, but I guess you didn't hear." She glanced down at the clothing in his hands. "Oh, how exquisite."

He handed her the items, then rose to his feet. "You can put them on. Just leave my robe in the bathroom."

She fingered the filigree and beads on the tunic, but her eyes never left his. "Whose are they?"

"My sister's." A shiver shook him. "Let me get a shower, then we'll talk. Tea's on the counter, should be cool enough to drink."

He gathered the things he needed while she changed, then headed into the bathroom when he heard her moving around in the kitchen.

Ten minutes later, he stepped out, showered, shaved and fully dressed. The smell of coffee permeated the air as he walked into the kitchen. Melena turned and handed him a mug of the hot brew. The sight of her in those clothes, her hair damp and curling, sent a jolt through him. He reached for the coffee with one hand, ran the other over her arm in a touch so soft he felt the tremble that shook her entire frame. She stepped away and sat at the table, her mug of tea cupped in both hands.

Garrett smiled. "Those look really good on you."

"They're stunning. I didn't know you had a sister."

"I don't talk about myself or my family much."

She smiled and his heart skipped a thud. "Not that we've had ample opportunity to really get to know one another."

He chuckled. "True."

Before he could say another word, awareness shivered up his spine, pricked his skin. He sensed her panic before his phone rang. He answered to a frantic Pat. "She's here. She's fine. I found her asleep on her feet, wading in the pond earlier. Yes, yes, I'll bring her right over."

He snapped the phone shut. "Looks like we're not going to have this conversation right now, either. Pat is beside herself. I've strict orders to get you there ASAP."

Melena rose and put their cups in the sink. "What about my gown?"

Garrett shrugged. "I can wash it and bring it over later or you can take it now. There are plastic bags in that drawer," he pointed as he spoke. "I'll get my boots on. But, Melena..."

He waited until her gaze met his again. "We will have this talk. Soon. And many more afterward."

A smile curved her lips and lit her eyes to a soft, emerald glow. Garrett walked away before he acted on the impulse pounding through his blood.

They arrived at the ranch to find Pat pacing the porch. She rushed out to meet Melena as she exited Garrett's truck and enfolded her in a bone-crushing hug. Words shuddered through her tense lips. "I woke up and you were gone. At first, I wasn't too worried but when I couldn't find you, I panicked."

"I'm sorry. I don't really know what happened." Both looked to Garrett.

He put an arm around each and urged them inside. They sat at the staff's table in the dining room. "I found her sleepwalking, or should I say sleep *diving*, in the pond. Said she was looking for Jon, that he'd told her to meet him there."

Melena shook her head. "That makes no sense, but..."

Garrett watched as she slowly unraveled, hyperventilating and shaking. Suddenly he knew. "Today's the anniversary, isn't it?" His stomach clenched at the devastation in her eyes and the sobs that racked her slender frame. Once Melena's bawling turned to soft, hiccupping sounds, Pat turned to him again.

"How did you know she was in trouble?"

"Bolted out of a sound sleep to a voice telling me to get to the ranch quick. Saw her before I got through the gate good. Scraped my truck all to hell and back. The gate's bent too, but still works."

Melena dragged a hand through her hair. "Guess now I have to worry about losing my mind or hurting myself on top of everything else."

Garrett shook his head. "Don't go there. Fear has a way of taking on a life of its own. Don't feed it. You've been under a lot of stress lately. The tea you drank earlier will help. I'll bring more over later. A cup before bed is all you need."

Pat raised an eyebrow at him. "What kind of tea?"

"An herbal mixture learned from the Shaman of my tribe."

"And these clothes?" Pat waved a hand at Melena.

"Belonged to my sister."

"You say that past tense."

"She passed away."

Empathy lit Pat's eyes. "Oh. I'm so sorry."

Garrett shrugged. "It was several years ago." He looked at his watch. "Folks'll be stirring around here soon, so I'd better get moving." He stood, reached down to caress Melena's cheek. "And you need to get some rest."

Melena rose from her seat also. "I'll go change and you can take these back with you." She turned and rushed up the stairs.

Garrett paled, swayed. Pat lurched to her feet, touched his arm. "You okay? You look as though you've seen a ghost."

He dry-washed his face with shaking hands. "For a moment, I did."

* * * * *

The next few days passed in a hectic whirl as the ranch staff prepared for the upcoming show. In town, the Utopia Arts & Crafts Guild geared up for the Annual Fall Fair. The day-long event served as a platform to exhibit the artists featured at the Crossed Penn later that same evening.

The phone never stopped ringing. Artists fretted as they chose and discarded which pieces they would showcase at the Fair and what would stay at the ranch. A steady parade of trucks loaded with food, equipment and artwork traveled into and out of the ranch gate. Everyone, even the guests, who were mostly artists' family members, pitched in to help. Melena hadn't heard whether her parents, children and grandchildren would be there for the show. She watched, waiting with hopeful anticipation, every time the door opened, then sighed in defeat when a family not her own walked through.

Each artist to be showcased at the ranch took turns working the booth in Utopia. The town square overflowed with vendors offering handmade crafts, homemade jellies and pies, metal and wood yard art. Flint knappers offered one of a kind knives and sharpening stones. Sculptors displayed pottery and ceramics. Designers set up purses, jewelry, quilts and crocheted items, hand crafted wind chimes and toys.

Melena couldn't get enough of the sights and sounds going on around her and snapped a steady stream of photographs. Her mind whirled with ideas on how to transfer all she experienced onto canvas or glass. And for a while, she forgot the disappointment that her family hadn't shown up yet. *If they even do.*

When her shift in town was up, Melena returned to the ranch to find Pat gone. She asked Anne if she knew where her friend had disappeared to.

"Said she had errands to run. She didn't know how long she'd be out, but she'll definitely be back before the show."

Melena shrugged, thanked Anne and mounted the stairs to her room. Once there, the nerves and fears she'd held at bay over the last few weeks rose to choke her. *Oh, God, what am I doing? I'm a housewife, mother and accountant. Not a gallery artist.*

Determined to overcome the onslaught of emotions battering away at her, Melena pulled out her sketch pad and set to work. Before long, the excitement she'd experienced earlier poured out onto pages and pages of colorful depictions. A knock on the door interrupted. "Who is it?"

"Garrett."

Melena scrambled from the bed and ran a brush through her hair, then opened the door.

"Hey."

Tension coiled the entire length of him.

"Are you okay?"

"I came to ask you the same thing."

Melena smiled. "I'm good. Almost gave in to the insanity a while ago but sketched it away."

"Okay, good. I'm about to head into town to clean up before the show. Guess I'll see you in a while."

Melena acknowledged his comment with a small nod. Concern curled through her when he hesitated and ran a hand through his hair. "Garrett, what's wrong?"

A low growl sounded in his throat. "I don't know why I let her talk me into this. It's going to be a disaster. I can feel it."

Melena stepped forward, laid her hand against the muscle in his cheek that jerked and spasmed as he ground his teeth, and felt him relax under her touch.

Frozen in the moment, they broke apart when someone stumbled up the stairs and gasped. "Mom?"

Melena turned as her daughter twirled on her heel and started back down the stairs. She bolted after her. "Kathryn!"

Her daughter swung through the kitchen doors then turned on Melena in an angry whirl. "How could you? We wanted to surprise you—well, I guess we did."

Pat, Jon Jr. and Anne rushed into the kitchen.

"What's going on?" Jon asked.

Kathryn flew into her brother's arms. "I s—s—saw her w—with a man."

"It's not what you think."

"He was in your bedroom!"

Melena took a deep breath and fought for calm as Anne and Pat slipped from the room. "He was not. We were in the hallway *outside* my bedroom." She turned an imploring gaze on Jon. "He's a friend and fellow artist, having a bad case of nerves. He just came to see how I was holding up."

Kathryn snorted in disbelief. Jon gave her a slight shake. "Stop it. Mom has the right to friends, even another love in her life."

"But it's barely been a year since daddy died! She couldn't bear to be home with us for the anniversary of his death. Right. Probably because of *him*."

Melena drew herself to her full five-foot, four-inch height. "How dare you, young lady. I loved your father! Love him still. You have no right to come here and stand in judgment over my decisions. When you've got your whole life figured out and perfected, *then and only then* can you tell me how to live mine."

She spun on her heel and marched out of the kitchen and ran straight into Garrett.

He put his hands on her arms to halt her mad dash up the stairs. "I'm sorry. I should have come down with you, tried to explain."

Melena shook her head. "No, *I'm sorry* for my daughter's rudeness and immaturity. I'm going upstairs to get ready. I'll see you in a while."

Garrett let her go and hesitated, unsure whether he should go into the kitchen and talk with her children as they continued to argue. Her son's firm stance on his mother's behalf convinced him the boy had things under control, so he left the two to their discussion. *For now.*

He walked out of the lodge, got into his truck and headed to his cabin in town.

* * * * *

Lit up like a beacon on top of the hill, the Crossed Penn blazed with light and color as people mingled, traipsing in, around and through the artwork displayed in clusters throughout the dining and lodge rooms.

Garrett approached the entrance with a mixture of anticipation and trepidation. For the past few days he hadn't been able to shake the feeling of dread, and premonition of something calamitous. The scene with Melena's children certainly qualified as disastrous, but Garrett's intuition told him more was on the way. He stepped through the door, stopped. His eyes searched for and found Melena surrounded by her children, Pat and a bubbly young woman.

"I'm so excited for you!" The girl exclaimed.

His pulse stuttered when Melena threw back her head and laughed. He moved forward, aware when the attention turned to him. Anne approached him with outstretched hands. He clasped them, bent his head for her kiss.

"How are you?" she whispered.

"I'm here," he mumbled, then shrugged when she asked if he was ready for the announcement. He glanced over at Melena, saw the kaleidoscope of emotions on her face and in her eyes.

"Give me a minute," he told Anne then walked to Melena's side. Her smile took his breath away.

"Hello, Ms. Rhyker. How're things going?"

Melena's excitement radiated through him when she touched his arm. "Hey, Garrett. It's wonderful. Please let me introduce you to my son, Jon, and daughter, Kathryn."

Garrett nodded at both, reached a hand toward Jon, relieved when the young man accepted the handshake without reservation. "Nice to meet you."

"And this is Missy." Melena drew his attention back by waving toward the young woman at her side. "She's an artist also, but currently works at a Visitor's Center in Louisiana."

Garrett took Missy's hand in his, tipped his hat while kissing her knuckles and felt her swoon. "Ma'am."

She giggled.

His spirits lifted a notch.

Anne walked up, hooked her arm around Garrett's and excused

them, then led him to the front of the room where a podium awaited. Getting everyone's attention, she cleared her throat as Bill joined them.

"Bill and I would like to thank each of you for coming out tonight. As promised, we have a very special guest in attendance. You've seen his work here, and in galleries across the world…" Her words trailed off as the murmurs started. She waited a beat then continued.

"Most of you have been asking for years to meet the artist behind the art. Tonight we're pleased to oblige you. Please give a huge welcome to my cousin, GS Whitecloud."

The room erupted in applause, then chaos as everyone talked at once, clamoring to get Garrett's attention.

He leaned toward the microphone and the room fell silent. He thanked Anne and Bill and proceeded to answer questions. He didn't know when the shivers started, followed by goose bumps. The atmosphere changed. Electrical pulses pricked his spirit. Apprehension rose to choke him when a voice rang out from the crowd.

"Hey, aren't you that guy who was involved in a drug sting that put that Indian, sorry, *Native American* drug lord in prison?"

"Excuse me?" Garrett tried to appear as though he misunderstood the question, while his mind scrambled to come up with an answer appropriate for the occasion.

"You heard me," the belligerent voice insisted.

Bill stepped up to the microphone. "Sir, the incident you're referring to happened a long time ago and has nothing to do with what's going on here tonight. I'm going to have to ask you to be silent or leave."

"Yeah, but didn't a DEA agent and a couple of women die in that?"

Bill started toward the man. Garrett's eyes sought Melena's and saw the shock on her face. His panicked gaze connected with Jon's as he too, walked toward the troublemaker. He watched, shaken, as the two converged on the guy and politely escorted him out of the room. Relief washed through him when Melena, flanked by Pat, reached his side.

Melena touched his arm and whispered his name. Garrett swallowed the thick coat of bile coating his throat, patted her hand then turned and stalked out of the room.

Chapter Fifteen

Garrett slipped up the stairs into a secluded alcove and stood at the window that overlooked the corral. He heard footsteps following and stiffened when Anne called his name in a soft tone. He refused to face her when she walked up behind and laid her hand on his shoulder.

"I'm sorry."

"I told you this would happen."

"I know you tried to warn me, but you can't run, can't hide forever."

"I don't see why not."

"Because the truth has a way of coming out and the truth will always set you free. You have nothing to be ashamed of about that time or what happened. You did your job. You put an evil, cruel, man away."

Her words halted at his indignant snort. "Yeah, and failed to protect two of the people I loved most in the entire world."

"You did your best, Garrett. Everyone knows you did, and no one blames you but yourself. You have to let go, forgive, and accept God's healing."

He cast off her hand with a nasty shrug. "Just leave me be."

Sorrow emanated from her. Garrett clamped down on the guilt swamping him when she turned with a deep sigh and walked away.

Within moments after Anne left, Melena came in.

"Anne shouldn't have bothered you."

"Anne didn't send me."

"So why are you here?"

Had she not seen the devastation in his eyes and on his face earlier, Melena would have taken offense at his demeanor. "I wanted to see if you're all right."

"I'm not sure how I am right now."

Concerned at the defeat in his tone, Melena placed her hand on his shoulder. "I know this isn't the time or place to discuss what happened, but I hate to think of you up here all alone. I need to get back down to the show. Why don't you come with me?"

"I'm sure my career is over."

"I wouldn't say that. There are more people down there who appreciate your work and are much more supportive of the artist they've come to know and love—despite never seeing you—than some strange man hell bent on starting a scene."

"What about your children?"

"My children are among them."

He turned to her then and her stomach clenched at the depth of shame, anger and sorrow in his expressive eyes. He removed her hand from his shoulder, closed the distance between them with a single step, and cradled her face in his hands. Melena leaned into him and lifted her face, anticipating his kiss. His lips trembled against hers, a soft brush of mouth on mouth as his hands trailed down her neck and shoulders then around her back to embrace her more fully.

Melena's hands glided up his arms and around his neck, fingers dipped into the dark depths of thick hair caressing his collar, then eased back as he ended the kiss in slow degrees. He buried his face in her hair. A shudder shook his entire frame.

"Thank you."

The ache in his voice fisted around her heart. Melena took a step back, held his hand in hers and together they went downstairs.

The sea of endless chatter ebbed and flowed as Garrett and Melena descended the stairs, then came to a near whisper when he reached Anne's side and gave her a fierce hug. He embraced Bill and turned to find Melena's son.

"Thank you for stepping up and helping avert a nasty scene."

The two shook hands but further conversation was halted when a couple approached Garrett asking for details about some of his work. Before long Melena's attention was drawn away from him as her own work was inquired about. As the night wore on, the amount of art on display diminished as people came and went, carrying their purchases with them. Other's left with receipts, packaging slips, and shipping arrangements complete. More than once Melena's senses would begin to hum. She'd glance around the room to find Garrett watching her, his eyes glistening with a host of emotions she dared not put a name to.

*****

Garrett trudged down the stairs the next morning in search of coffee. He'd succumbed to the insistent pleas of Anne, Melena and Pat and stayed here last night, instead of going to his cabin in town. He settled at the table of love with a warmed-over cup while waiting for the pot to brew. He glanced up when Kidd stumbled through the kitchen door with a groan.

"You all right?"

Kidd warmed a cup of leftover coffee in the microwave and

nodded. "The last couple of days have taken their toll."

Garrett grinned. "Too much for an old married man?"

"Ha ha."

Kidd's comical expression turned sober. "I heard what happened. Wish I'd been in here to toss the jerk out by the seat of his pants, with my boot aptly applied. Are you okay?"

Garrett shrugged. "Knew it'd come out sooner or later. Guess all there is to do now is wait out the storm."

"Well, you know you're not alone in this."

"That's right." A voice sounded from the stairs. Melena's son descended the staircase, pulled out a chair and joined them. "But I would like to know what the hell that was about, and how my mother fits into your life."

"Fair enough. Coffee first though." Garrett rose, went into the kitchen, poured three mugs of the fresh brew and brought them to the table.

"You might ought to wait and tell the story when everyone else is up. Otherwise you'll have to repeat it numerous times," Kidd advised.

"True," Jon chimed. "But my mother?"

Garrett cocked back in his chair, sipped his coffee and closed his eyes. The memory of his first meeting with Melena filled his mind and warmed the chill from his soul. "The first time I met her, I knew my running days were over. I know she's been through a lot with your father's death and I have no idea where our relationship will go. But know this. I will never dishonor or disrespect her or your father's memory."

Jon acknowledged the pledge with a nod, sipped his own coffee. "I just don't want to see her hurt. In any way."

"That's not in the plan either."

"It never is," Jon muttered.

"Right, but you can't protect her from life. She's a brilliant artist who needs to spread her wings and see where that talent takes her."

"And you intend to be with her while she figures that out?"

Garrett leaned over, put a hand on Jon's shoulder. "As long as she'll let me. And I'll do everything within my power to help her heal, and to guide, guard and protect her when we're together. In whatever capacity. You have my word on that."

Kidd's chuckle cut seriousness to the bone. "As a cowboy and a gentleman?"

Garrett threw back his head and laughed. "Yeah."

Later, when everyone had risen and were seated around the breakfast table, Garrett shared the events that culminated in his father, a drug lord, being sent to prison, and his subsequent years in the CIA.

"So, what the guy said last night is true?" Melena's daughter asked.

Garrett nodded, blinked to clear his blurred his vision and swallowed the knot in his throat. He dragged a hand over his chest where the bullet scars throbbed. "Yes. My mother and sister were killed in the shootout when my father held them hostage. My friend, a DEA agent, died trying to rescue them."

"Oh, my," Kathryn murmured, her voice tinged with sadness. A thick silence hung over the table, broken when she turned to Anne. "So, how are you two cousins?"

"Our mothers were sisters."

"When did you discover your gift for photography?" Melena wanted to know.

Anne laughed. "He's had a camera in his hands as far back as I can remember."

Garrett chuckled, glad he'd withstood the telling without a total meltdown. The compassion and affection in Melena's gaze encouraged him to relate how he'd grown from a wide-eyed child with a toy camera, to a man with a passion for still-life, compositional theory, patterns, symmetry and abstract.

As the day wore on, they moved from the table to the lodge room, talking while cleaning up from the night before. Conversation, mixed with stretches of silence or bouts of laughter, rang throughout the ranch house until lunchtime and continued over the meal. When afternoon rolled around and the time came for Jon, Kathryn and Missy to leave, Melena and Pat drove them to the airport.

Melena hugged each of them. "I'm so glad you came. Pat and I will be home in a few days."

Missy picked up her bag. "Y'all stop by the Visitor's Bureau on your way through."

"Take your time," Jon said.

Kathryn agreed. "Yeah. We're so proud of you, Mom. Love you."

Melena smoothed the dampness off her cheeks. "Love you too. Give the kids, Grams and Grandpa a hug for me."

"We will," they promised then stepped through security.

Melena and Pat were half-way back to the ranch when a text from Garrett came through on her phone. *Hey, pretty lady? Gonna be long?*

No. We're headed back now.

Okay. I need to head out to Arizona but wanted to see you before I leave.

Melena's excitement dived. She hadn't expected he would leave the ranch before she did. *At least I'll see him before we go back to our normal lives.*

If there is such a thing.

Chapter Sixteen

"Great show, Mel. What's next?"

Pat's question interrupted her musings. Melena smiled over at her. "Anne said this show is just the beginning but I'm not sure what happens next. I know this much, as wonderful as it all was, and is, I'm ready to be home with my family for a while."

"What about Garrett?"

"That's another situation I've no clue about. We care, but where it'll lead is anybody's guess."

Pat's sigh spoke volumes. "I just hope you don't rush into anything there. Take some time to enjoy this new phase in your life. Your talent and the opportunities it brings you."

"I don't plan to rush into anything, but neither do I want to spend my life alone." Melena let out a shaky laugh. "But we're getting way too far ahead of ourselves so let's not go there." Relief washed through her when the ranch gate came into sight.

Within minutes they'd parked and exited the car. In the lodge, they found Anne and Garrett deep in conversation. Both looked up at the tinkling of the bell on the door. Garrett pushed back from the table, rose and met them midway across the room. He embraced Pat.

"Heard you're heading off to Arizona," she remarked. "Be careful on the road."

"Yeah. Gotta go there for a bit. Y'all be careful going back to Mississippi too."

Pat murmured in agreement and joined Anne at the table.

Garrett took Melena's hand and walked with her into the lodge room. "Any idea when I can see you again?"

The tenderness in his gaze warmed her. "I'll let you know as soon as I know."

He raised her hand to his mouth, swiped a kiss over the back then placed her palm against his chest. He tucked a strand of hair behind her ear, cupped her head in his palm. "Then I guess this'll have to hold us over till then," he murmured, and lowered his lips to hers.

A soft sigh trembled through her as his heart thudded beneath her palm. Melena eased her hand around his waist and let herself sink into the kiss.

* * * * *

Melena pulled into the drive at her Mississippi home two days after she and Pat left the ranch. Instead of driving straight through, they'd spent the night in Louisiana. They stopped in to see Missy who was all atwitter and awhirl over the show, especially since Anne had invited her to send some of her artwork along with an application for scholarship for next year's retreat. Melena called her parents and children, unloaded her car then a settled in the tub for a nice, hot bath.

As the fragrant steam swirled around her, her thoughts filled with memories of Garrett and the intimate moments they'd shared. *Where was he? What was he doing? Why hadn't he called or texted?*

Unsure whether the attraction they shared was sheer magnetism or something deeper, she didn't have the nerve to be the first to initiate contact.

As if bidden by her thoughts, her phone dinged, signaling an incoming message.

Hey, pretty lady.

Melena's hands shook as she reached for the towel, dried them and picked up the phone. *Hey. I was just thinking of you.*

Only just?

She laughed out loud. *This time. How've you been?*

Good. What do you mean this time?

How could she tell him she'd thought about him almost constantly?

You've crossed my mind a time or two. She added a smiley face, winking emoji.

A moment later a broken heart appeared on her screen.

They texted a few more minutes. Garrett brought her up to speed with what he'd been doing since arriving at the reservation in Arizona and she told him of her trip home and Missy's news.

Great! Anne told me she thought Missy had talent.

Yeah. I'm so excited for her!

By the time their conversation ended, Melena's water had chilled and goose bumps covered her skin. She stepped out of the tub, wrapped a towel around her and walked into the bedroom. She reached for the lamp on her bedside table. Her hand smacked against something. *Ouch!*

She turned on the light and bent to pick up the picture frame which had landed on her foot.

Jon.

Melena sank onto her bed, slammed by a sudden realization. She hadn't thought about her husband in weeks. Clasping the photo to her breast, she curled up on the bed and wept.

* * * * *

As he made his way to the sweat lodge, Garrett's mind wandered back over his conversation with Melena. Their playful banter made him chuckle. Familiar sensations stole over him as he approached the wigwam. He hesitated, allowed his spirit to open. *I'm here, Lord. I'm willing. Speak to me as You will.*

Stepping out of his moccasins, Garrett crossed the threshold into the steamy room. His eyes adjusted to the dim recesses, lighted only by the heated coals in the center. His grandfather rested on his mat. The Shaman wasn't joining them tonight. Garrett dropped his towel on the bench, sat cross-legged on his own mat, and allowed his mind to empty.

How are you, my son?

The words entered his spirit. He answered his grandfather the same way. *I'm really good, Grandfather.*

You seem much more relaxed since your last visit. Happier. More at peace.

Unwilling to break the intimate silence, Garrett allowed his spirit to converse with his Grandfather's. *I am.*

I am at peace knowing this.

The two remained silent for a while as each immersed into their own spiritual journey. The more he allowed himself to relax, the more open Garrett's spirit became until it flew wild and free. Soaring through the past, hovering in the present, venturing into the future. He saw his sister, dressed in the native garb. She ran and laughed and danced. His mother too, appeared to him, peaceful and serene.

Forgive yourself. You've carried this burden too long.

The words seeped into his essence, vibrated at the core of his being. Garrett knew it was time, past time, to embrace them. As he surrendered, Melena appeared. And Jon. After seeing his son, there was no mistaking the man this time. Garrett allowed the vision to play out until she turned to him, her eyes filled with joy. And love.

She would be fine.

She would be his.

The rocks hissed. More steam rose, and with it, all the guilt from his soul. He reached for his towel, wiping sweat and tears from his eyes. For the first time in nearly two decades, Garrett felt almost whole. He knew forgiving his father would be the final stitch in repairing the rents in his heart but couldn't fathom that just yet. *One hurdle at a time.*

His grandfather rose, then bent to wrap a small blanket around Garrett's shoulders.

"You've done well, my son. What was your turning point?"

"I agreed to reveal my identity at the art show this year."

"Ah, so your gift has made room for you."

Garrett frowned. "What?"

His grandfather smiled. "Search your great book," he said then walked out of the lodge.

* * * * *

Melena propped her feet up with a sigh. *Boy, am I t-i-r-e-d.* The past two weeks had either flown or dragged by, depending on her mood and what she had on the agenda for the day. Since her return from the ranch after the art show, she'd thrown herself into painting and cleaning. Closets, cabinets, attic. She'd gone through Jon's clothes with no lack of anguish. His photograph still graced the table by her bed, and she talked to him often. Sometimes with grief and anger and sheer agony. Mostly with love and acceptance. Pat came by two days ago on her way out of the country on a mission trip. God willing, her friend would be back for Christmas and New Years.

She and Garrett talked or texted almost daily. Sometimes a full conversation, others a brief, fun interaction. Occasionally a single message would pop up on her screen, followed by an emoji that made her sigh with longing or laugh with joy. Melena scrolled back through his latest correspondence.

Hey, Melena, hope all is well with you. May be out of touch for a while. Traveling. Working.

He'd sent her a picture of a gorgeous sunset cast over water and trees and mountains. *Oh, to have stood at his side when he captured this glorious scene.*

Melena closed her eyes, allowed her thoughts to wander and suddenly she was beside him. Standing on a precipice. Crossing a meadow of wildflowers. Hiking a through a shadowed forest. Trekking through—

The phone shrilled. Melena jerked upright, her pulse chattering. "Hello?"

"Mom!" Kathryn's voice rang over the airwaves. "Turn on the news."

"What?"

"Are you home?"

"Yes."

"Turn on the news!"

Melena fumbled in her haste to find the remote and turn the TV on. There on her screen was a picture of Garrett that night at the ranch next to video replays from years ago. The newscaster's voice echoed in the empty room. "Penn, Whitecloud's manager, declined an interview, saying she hadn't been in touch with him for several days and had no idea how to reach him." He looked into the camera as if he could see the viewers through the lens, his eyebrow arched, gaze intense. His voice lowered to a dramatic timbre. "Has he gone into hiding? Again?"

"Oh, my goodness," Melena murmured.

"Have you heard from him?"

Before she could answer her daughter, the phone beeped indicating another call. "Hang on."

Melena glanced at the caller ID to see Anne's number flashing. "That's Anne, honey. I've got to take it. I'll talk to you later." She switched over before Kathryn could respond.

"Anne?"

Before Anne could utter a word, Melena's house phone rang. "Hang on!"

"Hello?"

Jon's voice thundered over the line. "Mom, did you see the news?"

"Yes, honey. I have Anne on my cell phone. Let me call you back."

She hung up with him and addressed Anne again. The phone beeped. Kidd's number flashed on the screen. Her house phone rang.

"Just stop!" Melena screeched and threw the cell phone. She picked up the house receiver, hit the 'end call' button and tossed it in the corner then covered her ears with trembling hands.

Is he all right? Will I ever see him again?

Chapter Seventeen

Melena had no idea how long she sat there, rocking with fear and uncertainty, when her son and daughter entered the house. Jon put his hands on her shoulders, gave a slight shake.

"Mom?"

"Oh, Jon! What if he just disappears or something's happened to him?"

Jon helped her to her feet, escorted her into the kitchen and pulled out a chair for her. Kathryn picked up the phones and joined them.

"Have you heard from him in the last few days?"

Melena nodded. "He texted me."

Jon scrolled through her messages until he found the one she meant. "Doesn't sound like a man who's gone into hiding or has no intention of contacting those he cares about. Damn media circus."

The phone rang. Jon turned the screen to where she could see who called. Melena grasped it like a lifeline. "Garrett!"

Her entire body sagged with relief when his chuckle sounded in her ear. "Hey, there."

Her panic must have registered because "What's wrong?" immediately followed the greeting.

Somewhere in the midst of her babbling about the news report she heard him curse.

"I'm catching the next flight out. I'll call you when I land." He hung up before she could say more.

Melena set her phone down, winced at the cracked screen and

accepted the glass of wine her daughter had poured. She sipped while the kids fended calls from her friends at the ranch and family here. Pat called. And Missy. After the hubbub settled, her children sat at the table with her. Kathryn reached for her hand. Melena clasped it and held out the other one for Jon.

"Thank you so much for coming. I'm sorry I fell apart like that." She put her head down, still shaken. And afraid. *Oh Lord, they'll think I've lost my mind.*

"We just want to know you're okay," Jon said.

Kathryn murmured in agreement.

"I'm fine. It's been a hectic couple of weeks. I've been cleaning and sorting and trying to paint. Create is a better word, I guess. The phone and emails haven't stopped with reports from the show and links and clippings of reviews. But nothing like this. Not until today. Seeing him wheeled out on that gurney after being shot just threw me for a loop. And then the way he looked at that trial..." Melena swallowed the thick coat of bile clogging her throat.

"You really care about him, don't you?" Her daughter wanted to know.

"Yes. I know it seems crazy. Sometimes even *I* don't understand how I can care so much when we barely know each other."

"Don't you think it's kinda soon to be in a relationship?" Jon asked, then held up his hand when her head jerked up, eyes narrowed. "I just don't want to see you hurt, Mom. It's obvious he's got a past filled with who knows what sort of baggage. Dad's barely been gone a year. I'm worried you're reading more into this than there is and leaving yourself open for more heartache."

Melena acknowledged his concern with a nod. "I hear what you're saying, honey, but I have no idea how to alleviate your fears. I only know what I feel. I never figured I'd be in such a position at this point in my life."

She released his hand, took another sip of her wine and smiled when Kathryn topped it off. "It's hard when you've got your whole life planned out. Where you'll go, what you'll do and how. Then BAM! Everything changes. You fumble around for a while. Lost. Alone. Unsteady."

The tremble of her hand amplified her statement. Melena put the glass down and clasped shaking fists in her lap. "God, the unsteady part is so long. So difficult. Half the time I still don't know if I'm coming or going. You second-guess everyone. Everything. Each decision and every emotion. Weighing what you would or should do, against what you would have done, what you want to do. And listen to all of the well-meaning voices instead of your own soul. Fear and uncertainty are constant companions, coloring every thought. Every desire and dream...when you dare to dream."

She knuckled a tear off her cheek. "I never imagined I'd be capable of the kind of art that has come through me these past months. Certainly didn't think anything I'd done or would ever do, would be gallery-worthy. This is new to me, too. I'm doing my best to navigate through it all."

"Do you think this with Garrett will last? Be a permanent thing?"

Melena winced at the throb in her daughter's voice. "I don't know that either, sweetie. We may never be more than friends and colleagues. All I do know is that I enjoy his company. I admire his talent and I care about him. Anything beyond that, beyond tomorrow or next week is still wrought with doubt and guilt and confusion. It's all so exhausting."

Jon's cell phone rang. By his end of the conversation, Melena knew her daughter-in-law was the caller. When he hung up, she reached for his and Kathryn's hands again. "Go home to your families. Give them hugs for me. I'll be fine."

"You sure? We don't want to leave you here alone."

Oh, but I need to be alone, Melena thought, but before she could address her daughter, her cell phone rang. Garrett's name flashed on the screen. Melena picked it up, accepted the call. "Hey, you landed already?"

"No, damn it. I can't catch a flight out until tomorrow. Bad weather. I saw a replay of that news report. Are you okay?"

"I'm fine. Sorry I was so panicked earlier. So you'll be flying out tomorrow?"

"I'm going to drive back. I talked to Anne. She's swamped Thanksgiving week, so I promised I'd help out. You gonna be there?"

"No, I'm sure we'll have Thanksgiving here."

"Oh. Well, maybe you can come up after."

The disappointment in his voice wound through her. "We'll see."

He promised to give her a call the next day, then hung up.

Jon rose. "I take it he's okay?"

Melena and Kathryn vacated their seats and the three made their way to the door. "Yeah. Leaving Arizona tomorrow and driving back to Texas. Seems the ranch is booked solid Thanksgiving week so he's going back to help. We are going to have dinner here, aren't we?"

Kathryn nudged her brother. "Why don't we get together on Sunday, then if you're needed at the ranch, you can be there for them?"

"Great idea," Jon agreed.

Melena hugged her children while sending up a silent prayer of thanks that they were so gracious and understanding. After they left, she called Anne and arranged to be at the ranch Thanksgiving week.

On Sunday evening, after a lovely lunch with her family and lots of hugs and kisses from her grandchildren, Melena headed for Utopia. As usual, she spent the night in Louisiana and then continued to the Crossed Penn on Monday. She'd asked Anne to keep her arrival a secret and looked forward to surprising her friends. She timed her entrance for right after dinner was served, but before the hayride. Garrett, who never sat with his back to the door, or a room for that matter, was the first to see her come in. His entire face lit up and set a horde of butterflies bouncing off her ribcage. He catapulted from his chair and in three long strides, swept her up in his arms and twirled her around.

"I didn't think I'd see you for another week or so."

Melena laughed. "We celebrated yesterday so I could come up today."

Her heart tripped over itself at the intensity of his gaze and the joy in his eyes.

She'd barely gained her feet when the entire staff rushed to embrace her also.

Laughing and talking all at once, they hustled her to the table, anxious to hear what she'd been up to the past three weeks. She answered their questions while each finished their meals, then went with Garrett and Kidd on the hayride.

Chapter Eighteen

Garrett switched places with Kidd for the hayride so Melena could sit with him in the truck. He didn't want her too far out of his sight. Or reach. He'd tempered his response when she showed up at the ranch, but now he wanted her alone. In his arms.

"Anne's got a room for you?" His heart skipped a thud when she smiled.

"Yeah. Last minute cancellation or something."

He ran a finger down her arm, clasped her hand in his and raised the knuckles to his lips. "You could always stay with me."

A visible tremble coursed through her. Her skin warmed beneath his hand; cheeks turned a lovely rose color. She stuttered then cleared her throat.

"I'm not sure I'm ready for that yet."

A low chuckle rumbled from his chest. "As long as I got'cha thinking about it, I'm good. You could come visit a while though. I'm done when the hayride is over."

She laid her cheek against his upper arm. A sweet, innocent gesture that set need surging through him like a tidal wave. Garrett rubbed his lips over her head and smelled the tantalizing scent of lavender and coconut in her hair. Releasing her hand, he put his arm around her shoulder and cuddled her to his side.

The hayride over, he parked the truck and hay wagon beneath the shed then helped Melena out. They walked hand in hand to her car, where he unloaded her suitcase and carried it up to her room.

She opened the door and allowed him to enter before her. He put the suitcase down and turned to her. She avoided his touch, lifted a beguiling gaze to his.

"Can I take a rain check on going to your house? It's so late, getting dark and I've been on the road for hours already today."

Garrett swallowed his disappointment. *Be patient.* The words echoed through his spirit. He closed the distance between them and took her hands in his. "Can I stay with you a while if I promise to behave? I want…I *need* to hold you."

Indecision warred with pleasure in her eyes. Garrett allowed her only a moment to refuse then moved closer, cupped her face in his hands and lowered his mouth to hers. A relieved sigh shuddered through his lips, as though he'd been dying of thirst and found relief in the sweet nectar of her mouth. He picked her up, sat in the huge winged-back chair in the corner and snuggled her to his chest.

* * * * *

Melena awoke the next morning tired and aching. Sleep, when she finally fell asleep, was neither deep nor restful. From the moment Garrett left, she'd been haunted by too many dreams, too many emotions. Oh, he'd been the perfect gentleman. They'd laughed and talked, sharing bits and pieces of their lives and what had transpired for each after the show. When she'd all but fallen asleep with her head on his shoulder, he set her on her feet, kissed her goodnight, then left.

While she washed her face, brushed her teeth and hair, and dressed for bed, the sweetness of their time together warmed her through and through. But somewhere in the night, memories of Jon, her son's concerns, daughter's initial shock at seeing her with Garrett and Pat's little pep talk about her sex life or the possibilities thereof, wove through her dreams. Everything jumbled together in vignettes that made her body ache and heart weep.

Pushing the covers back, she padded into the bathroom and stood a long time in the shower, hoping the hot, pulsating spray would clear the cobwebs from her mind. One look in the mirror and she fought not to break down and cry at the raw emotions reflected in her eyes. *What am I doing? I'm not ready for this. Why did I even think I needed or wanted to be here?*

Questions rolled around in her head until she thought she'd be sick. As quickly as possible she dressed, braided her hair and escaped the walls closing in on her. She slipped into the kitchen, put a pot of coffee on to brew and put away the dishes that were left out to dry the night before. She wasn't sure exactly where she'd be working the most this week, so just did what she saw needed to be done.

Before long, the employees and guests began stirring around her. As busy as they were, avoiding direct contact with Garrett wasn't difficult. Except at mealtimes, he was out in the corral with Kidd leading trail rides and tending to horses. Obviously, her emotional turmoil had been evident to only her because no one mentioned the wild look she'd seen in her reflection that morning.

When dinner was over and the hayride underway, Melena helped Bob clean up and prep for the next day's meals. Anne halted her on the way to her room.

"What time did you get started this morning? I hadn't put out a timecard for you yet, so we need to pencil in your hours for today."

Melena shrugged. "Early. I was in the kitchen before Bob came in."

Concern clouded Anne's eyes. "I figured you'd sleep late after making that drive up. Are you okay? You look more than exhausted."

Melena shook her head. "Just the opposite. I didn't sleep well at all last night. Too much excitement, I guess."

"Well, I'll put you down for twelve hours today. That's what our employees average this week anyway. Get some rest tonight. You're going to need it."

Melena thanked her and headed up to her room. She'd barely finished washing away the grit and grime from her day's activities when a knock sounded on her door.

"Who is it?" She asked, even though she knew. She could feel his magnetic presence through the thin wood that separated them.

"Garrett."

She opened the door.

His greeting froze on his lips. His gaze swept over her in a look so blatantly male, it left her breathless and blushing to the roots of her dark hair. A shiver trembled through her. Her pulse jumped into high gear. *Will I ever get used to the way he looks at me?*

"You look refreshed."

Melena tugged the robe tighter around her waist, let out a short laugh. "Bull. What I look is exhausted."

He chuckled and caressed her cheek. "Gorgeous. Know what you need? A moonlight stroll and a glass of wine."

"What I need is a good night's rest." Melena hated the disappointment that flashed in his eyes. But as memories emerged from her wild imaginings the night before, she was too vulnerable to be alone with him, especially with moonlight and wine. "I'm sorry,

Garrett. I didn't sleep well last night. Thanks for the invitation though."

"You still have some of that tea I gave you?"

She nodded. "In my overnight bag."

He held out his hand until she gathered the herbal concoction and brought it to him. While he went downstairs to prepare her a cup, she changed into pajamas. She unbraided her hair, mixed a couple of drops of lavender and coconut oil between her palms and worked it through the coarse tresses. She'd just fished her brush out of the vanity drawer when he knocked again.

"Come in."

He walked in, held out the tea and took the brush from her. "Let me."

The husky timbre of his voice feathered over her like a caress. Melena's hand shook when she accepted the mug, but she curled up on the foot of her bed while he pulled the chair closer.

"Who's counting?"

"Just brush."

His chuckle filled her with a warm glow. In long, soothing strokes, he ran the bristles through her hair until it lay in a silken mass down her back. He put the brush down, swept the hair out of his way and pressed his lips to the nape of her neck.

"Sshhh," he whispered when she started to protest. "I'm just going to hold you until you finish your tea."

Melena relaxed against him and they sat in silence while she sipped the remaining liquid from her cup. Within moments of drinking the last drop, her eyes drooped. Garrett shifted her in his embrace, pressed a kiss to her forehead and whispered goodnight.

By the time she'd settled beneath the covers, he'd returned her brush to the bathroom and put the chair where it belonged. He picked up the empty cup and left the room, turning off lights and locking the door on his way out.

* * * * *

When Sunday rolled around and the last guest checked out, the entire staff reclined around the lodge room. Garrett and Kidd had turned the horses loose. Melena and Marcey helped Bob until the kitchen sparkled. Anne insisted the housekeeping could wait a couple of days and that they all take a break. Garrett and Kidd each sprawled out on a couch, Kidd with his head in Marcey's lap. Melena chose a huge, comfy chair and propped her feet on the matching ottoman. Bob occupied another chair. Shelley locked the office and sank into the one remaining. Anne and Bill walked in from the kitchen carrying a tray of champagne, orange juice and flutes.

Garrett arched an eyebrow at his cousin. "Kinda early to start drinking, don't'cha think?"

Anne laughed. "Never too early to show our appreciation and drink a toast to you guys. You all are champs in our book." So saying, she poured the mimosas and Bill handed them out.

Melena hesitated. "I probably shouldn't if I'm going to start the drive home this afternoon."

Garrett swung into an upright position. "You're not leaving today?" Although he hadn't gotten her alone at his house this week, their nightly visit at the close of the day had sufficed. But now, he wanted her all to himself.

"I thought I'd at least get a few miles behind me."

Anne handed her a glass. "Maybe you ought to wait and leave early in the morning."

Everyone chimed their agreement.

"That way we don't have to worry about you traveling so late. Especially knowing how tired you must be," Marcey added. Her tone and expression pleaded their case.

Melena capitulated with a sigh, took the drink. "I guess you're right."

Anne raised her glass. "To the best employees, and friends, we've ever known."

Everyone cheered, took a sip and let out audible sighs of appreciation.

"I'll have you all know, I'm very proud of my husband." Marcey's announcement was met with raised brows. "He didn't flirt with a single woman."

"You didn't see him out on the trail."

"Shut up, Garrett," Kidd muttered. He gazed up at his wife. "He's just pulling your chain."

The teasing turned to laughter as everyone shared funny stories and antidotes of the week past. As the atmosphere quieted, each immersed in their own thoughts, Garrett put down his glass, rose and held a hand toward Melena. "Take a walk?"

She groaned. "My feet can't handle a walk."

He chuckled and pulled her out of the chair. "A drive, then."

"Remember, dinner at seven," Anne reminded.

Whenever possible, their custom was to treat the staff to dinner at a local restaurant after a busy week. They deserved a meal they didn't have to cook or clean up afterward. Garrett waved in acknowledgement and led Melena out to his truck.

"Where are we going?"

Garrett shrugged. "Anywhere I can get you alone. Away from people and their demands."

He glanced over, caught the flash of excitement followed by trepidation on her face. "Stop that."

"What?"

"You're thinking too much. I'm not going to pressure you into anything you're not ready for or don't want. Haven't I proved that this week?"

He could have kicked himself when something akin to a sob passed through her tense lips.

"Yes. You've been nothing but chivalrous all week. It's not you, Garrett, it's me. I don't know what I want much less what I'm ready for."

Liar. A voice screamed in her head. *You know exactly what you want. It's been how long since you've been held? Touched. Loved.*

Too long, she admitted silently.

Pat's voice joined in the fray... *"When a man and woman respect and care about each other, sex is a natural extension of the relationship."*

But do we even have a relationship? *We care about and respect each other as people and artists, and there's no doubting the attraction between us, but does all that constitute a relationship?*

Uncertainty mixed with panic knotted her stomach. Melena pressed a hand against her midsection and prayed Garrett couldn't read her mind. His voice drew her out of the argument in her head. "I'm sorry. Did you say something?"

"I asked if you wanted anything special to drink. I don't have much more than mineral water at my house. Or we can make tea if you'd like."

"A cup of tea would be nice."

In the time it took Garrett to park the truck in front of his cabin, climb out and walk around to open her door, Melena prayed more fervently than she had in months.

Chapter Nineteen

Melena wrapped her hands around the warm mug and took a deep inhale of the soothing scent wafting from the cup. "How can I be sure you didn't put something in here that'll make me succumb to your every whim?"

"Darn it!" Garrett snapped his fingers for emphasis. "I knew I forgot something."

The chuckle escaped. Melena's cheeks warmed. She raised her gaze to meet the laughter in his eyes.

Garrett sat across from her then reached out to caress her face.

"When the time comes for us to make love, I won't need to doctor your tea. The passion latent within you astounds me. I'm sure it'll take the rest of my life to tap into it. Draw it out. Share it with you."

The tenderness in his touch, in his gaze, *in those words*, moved Melena to the very core of her being. Her pulse scrambled, heart beat so hard it was a wonder her chest didn't burst wide open. He inched toward her, whispered her name in that beautiful, guttural tone, and covered her lips in a kiss so gentle, so sweet.

Open for me.

Melena felt the request clear to her soul, could do nothing less. *God help me, I love him.*

She didn't protest when Garrett lifted her in his arms. Couldn't. The realization that she loved him rendered her helpless to everything but the intensity of emotions coursing through her entire body.

He carried her into the bedroom, laid her on the huge king-sized bed and removed her shoes and socks. Massaged her feet. Melena nearly arched off the bed when he pressed his lips to her instep. His fingers caressed her ankles, moved up her calves. Kneading. Stroking.

She opened her eyes, could barely see him through the hazy cloud blinding her vision. The air around them vibrated. Sparks rose with goose bumps on her skin. Soft, sweet words of love and desire bathed her senses in light and color. The mattress shook when he toed his boots off and shifted his length more fully against her. His hands never stopped moving, words never stopped flowing, binding her to him—heart, mind, body. Soul.

Melena felt the change the moment he opened her blouse and halted at the wedding rings nestled between her breasts. Before she could protest, he moved the gold bands aside, replaced them with his lips. Tears welled up in her eyes, clogged her airways. Spilled over. Garrett buried his hands in her hair, kissed her cheeks, her eyelids.

"Stay with me," he whispered, swallowing her denial with his lips.

A loud clatter sounded outside the window. *Clash! Scrape!*

"What?"

"Sshh!" His edict screeched through the quiet.

Melena gasped when he rolled away from her, reached into the bedside table and pulled out a gun. She scrambled into a sitting position. He pressed a finger to her lips then his own, rose with absolute silence, walked to the window and peered through the blinds.

Shit! Garrett didn't know whether to laugh or shoot the damn deer.

He blew out a frustrated breath, annoyed that their moment had been shattered by a rutting buck and an instinct that had guided and guarded him his entire life.

"What is it?" Fear trembled in Melena's voice.

He grinned over at her, motioned for her to join him, and cautioned her to be quiet. Melena eased from the bed and tiptoed to his side. A smile bloomed on her face.

"He's magnificent. Is that the same deer you created that incredible piece around?"

"One of them."

"Wow!"

A moment later she looked up at him, her gaze wary. "You sleep with a gun by your bed. Is there anything from your past that can come back to haunt you? Us? Hurt my children or grandchildren?"

Garrett hugged her to his side and kissed the top of her head. "No."

"How about I warm up that tea?"

"Sounds good. I'll be there in a minute."

Melena went into the kitchen. He heard the microwave door pop open. The glass turntable clinked when she put the cups in.

"Don't nuke them!" he called out then strode in. "Sorry. Didn't mean to yell. Radiation from the microwave will kill the nutritional qualities of the herbs."

He dumped the contents of both mugs into a single glass container, added another tea bag and put the kettle on to boil. His phone dinged. A text from Kidd came through. *Heading to the restaurant a little early. Join us ASAHP.*

Dinner with the crew was a lively affair, filled with laughter and fun. Often throughout the evening Garrett reached over and touched Melena. Her hand, her knee. A brush of his knuckles across her cheek. A caress of her hair. Subtle assurance that regardless of what went on around them, she was uppermost in his mind. When the meal ended and everyone groaned because they'd overindulged, he pushed back from the table and offered her his hand. "I'll take you home."

"I'm sure I can catch a ride with someone. There's no need for you to drive out to the ranch and then back into town."

He shook his head and helped her to her feet. "You dance with the one who brought you. I'll take you home."

"That's right," Kidd interjected. "Neither a gentleman nor a cowboy would let a lady catch her own ride."

Melena laughed with the rest of them and allowed him to take her arm and escort her out of the restaurant.

"Sure you don't want to stay with me? I'll bring you home in the morning."

Pleasure tingled through him when Melena smiled and ran her fingertips over the five o'clock shadow on his face.

"Tempting though that is, I think I need to pass. I still have to pack and get ready to leave tomorrow."

"Already told you, you think too much." The laughter in his voice took any trace of sting out of the words.

She chuckled.

"Seriously, though, why don't you stay a couple of days?" Garrett opened himself and allowed the depth of his feelings to permeate his aura, flow toward her. *Open for me.* She trembled beside him with a gasp. He turned the truck toward his cabin.

Nerves fluttered in Melena's throat. *What is happening here? I can hardly breathe. He's infiltrating every cell of my body. Of my mind. Of my every sense.*

She moved away from him, closer to the door and shook off the thoughts. "I'm sorry. I can't do this. Please, just take me to the ranch."

The change in atmosphere was acute. A tearing away. One heart from the other.

"I don't understand what you're so afraid of."

Disappointment bordering on despair colored his tone. Melena struggled not to cry. "Neither do I."

Relief washed through her when he made a U-turn and pointed the truck in the direction of the ranch.

They rode the entire way in silence. When he parked, Melena reached for the door handle only to be stopped by a firm, but gentle hand.

"Mind if I visit with you while you pack?"

The hope in his eyes, in his voice, seared the denial on her tongue. Her lips curved. "That would be lovely."

She waited for him to climb out of the truck, walk around and open her door, then took his hand and held it against her cheek. "Thank you for being so patient, so understanding."

He tugged their clasped hands to his mouth, kissed her palm. "I said I'd never push or force you. I'm doing my best to honor that promise. If I have, in any way, it's been unintentional."

They went inside and up the stairs. Garrett took the key from her and opened the door to her room. A huge bouquet of flowers took up the entire surface of her bedside table. Melena picked up the vase, buried her nose in the soft blooms and absorbed the sweet scent.

"I wonder who these are from." He eyed her, one brow arched.

She laughed at the comical expression and tone, picked up the envelope that lay beneath the vase and opened it. And nearly dropped the flowers along with her jaw when two fat checks filled her palm. Garrett took the flowers and put them down while she unfolded the note.

Congratulations on your success at the show and thank you for helping out this week. Love, Anne and Bill.

"My first commissions check." She showed the amount to Garrett. "I'm an artist!"

She flung herself into his arms, laughing and crying all at once.

He twirled her around, kissed her then chuckled. "Of course you're an artist. Anne wouldn't have showcased you if you weren't!"

"I know, but I never dreamed...."

Her eyes welled. Happy tears mixed with sad. "It only took my husband dying to find out."

Sadness won out over joy. Garrett gathered her to his chest and let her cry. "You must think I'm an idiot, blubbering all over the place."

He smoothed the hair off her cheeks then whisked the moisture away with his lips. "I think you're adorable."

Melena nestled her head against his shoulder. "Thank you. You're so sweet. You're probably used to big royalty checks by now."

He laughed. "Never gets old. You need to copy and frame that."

"Great idea!"

Later, when her suitcases were all packed and Garrett got ready to leave, she walked with him down the stairs. He stopped when she reached the last one, turned, eye-level with her. "I'm thinking I'll hit the road tomorrow too."

"Arizona?"

He nodded. "Among other places. I tend to get up early so I may not see you. Besides, I don't know how many more goodbyes I can handle. Watching you walk away. Not knowing when I'll see or hear from you."

Melena wrapped her arms around his neck, leaned into his kiss and whispered, "Soon."

Chapter Twenty

Jubilation mixed with agony accompanied Melena the entire trip home. She kept the radio turned up loud to avoid thinking about what transpired between her and Garrett. As usual, she stopped in to see Missy and shared the excitement of her success with the budding artist. Encouraged her.

"I sure hope I get that scholarship. I certainly can't afford the retreat on my own. Yet."

"Have faith and you will." Melena loved her confidence and enthusiasm and vowed silently to be sure Missy attended the retreat next year. Their conversation brought a whole slew of questions to mind.

Would she and Garrett be back for the retreat? Back to work? Would she be on tour? How would Garrett, the ranch, her art, a *tour* mesh with her current life?

She arrived home late Monday evening, exhausted. After pouring a glass of wine, she texted her children, Anne, and Garrett, then relaxed in a hot bath.

The next morning, she awoke to crushing oppression. She picked up Jon's photo off the table, clutched it to her chest. *Oh, God, WHY?* She curled into a tiny ball and wept.

Her phone rang. She glanced at caller ID, sniffled, smiled then answered with as much enthusiasm in her voice as she could summon. "Hey, friend. Where are you? When are you coming home?"

Pat's chuckle sounded over the line. "On my way from Guatemala.

Be there in a couple of days. Are you okay?"

Anguish welled up and poured out before she could stop it. "I don't know! Got my commissions check from the show. It's huge, Pat. More than I ever dreamed possible. I should be ecstatic, but I'm not. I feel so...empty!"

"Did something happen at the ranch? With Garrett?"

Melena put the frame down. No way could she tell Pat about Garrett while holding Jon's picture. She climbed out of bed and padded toward the kitchen. "We had a lovely week. Busy. Crazy busy. But fun. He visited me every evening. Then..." She hesitated, not sure how much she should reveal.

Didn't matter. Pat knew. Melena heard her quick oath. "You slept with him?"

"No. We had a few intimate moments. Came close. But no. Now I'm so torn. I realized how much I do care about him. Love him even. But here, it all seems so surreal. Nothing's the same. This house is not the same. I'm not the same. I can't do this!"

"Yes. You can. Calm down. He didn't pressure you, did he?"

Concern filled her voice. Melena smiled to herself. *My warrior friend.* "No, he's too much a gentleman to do that. But what we shared...it's so strange. Like I could feel his very essence, his spirit...I don't know. This sounds crazy but I felt as though he were consuming me. But not in a bad way."

Pat's sigh shivered through Melena. "I knew this was coming. I only hoped it wouldn't be so soon."

"What do you mean?"

"I sensed his feelings for you the first time we met, confirmed them over the pond incident. Despite the teasing and flirting, Garrett had a deeper bond with you than someone who'd known you a mere couple of months. A soul tie."

"How is that possible?"

"We're spiritual beings, Mel, and ultimately we're all connected. Some call it spiritual, others energetic, but on some level, we're linked, especially to those with whom we're on an intimate level. That's why you feel things when you meet someone, sense their joy or pain, fear or have caution around them for no reason. Or have a sense of déjà vu in a place you never recall visiting...."

A soft curse echoed over the line. "My flight's being called, Mel. Hang in there, I'll be home soon, and we'll talk. Meanwhile, spend some quality time alone, just you and God. He'll give you wisdom and understanding. Gotta run!"

She hung up before Melena could respond. Over the next couple of days, she did as Pat suggested. Fasting and praying, she sought answers. She read, researched, wrote and painted and came to a deeper understanding of what was happening within, and to, her on a spiritual level. How to tap into her God-given intuition and to discern what was right for *her,* on a personal—physical, spiritual and emotional—level. Before Pat even arrived home, Melena knew it was time to have another tête-à-tête with her family. She called and invited them and her parents to have dinner with her.

After the meal had been served, kitchen cleaned and kids tucked safely in the den watching cartoons, Melena prayed for the words to express what she had determined. "I can't go on like this. I'm going to sell the house."

As expected, opposition came from all directions.

"What?"

"But we've lived here all our lives!"

"Don't sell your house. In time, you'll feel differently."

Melena waited until the emotions settled then looked each family member in the eye, held their gaze a moment, then continued. "I understand what you're all saying, and I appreciate your opinions on the matter, but I have to do what's best for *me*."

"Why do you feel it's best?" Jon asked.

Glad he had been the one to ask, she took his hand, reached for Kathryn's. "It's hard to start a new life when the old one fills every nook and cranny of my environment."

"You're not thinking of moving to Texas, are you?" The fear in her daughter's voice hit hard. That's exactly what she had been thinking. Melena took a deep breath. "Yes, I've considered it. But I don't really want to be that far from you all and the kids. I don't have all the answers yet, but I know I need a change if I'm going to keep moving forward with my life."

"Does Garrett have anything to do with this?" Her son asked.

Melena shrugged. "No." She hesitated, tuned in to her innermost being. "Maybe. I don't know what our future holds or even if there is an 'our' in my future. But I do know I can't picture him, or *any* man, here where I've shared so much love and so many memories with your father."

Her father shifted, reached over and touched her shoulder. "Why don't you wait another year. Go on your tour. See how this new relationship pans out and then see how you feel?"

"Or at least wait until after the holidays to make such a drastic decision," her mother added.

"Yeah," her father interjected. "Besides we haven't even met this guy."

Melena smiled at his tone, but the thought of another Christmas in this house grated on her volatile emotions. She rolled her shoulders, bit her lip and capitulated.

Two days later a knock sounded on her door, followed by the doorbell. Melena grabbed a cloth, dabbed it in turpentine, then dropped her brush in the jar.

"Coming!" she hollered, wiping her hands as she made her way to the foyer. She glanced out the window, opened the door with a smile and pulled Pat into a dancing hug.

"You're back! I figured you'd be around sooner. Worried a little when I didn't hear from you, but with the weather reports, figured you got delayed or switched flights, had no signal or something."

Pat laughed. "Yeah, the joys and hiccups of traveling."

"Come in, come in! Can I get you something? Coffee? Tea? Juice?"

"I didn't interrupt your creative flow, did I?"

Melena smiled. "No. Finished the current work. Want to see it?"

"Of course."

They went into the room Melena had turned into a makeshift studio. She waited while Pat examined the painting.

"Charming, Mel. Where did you see this place?"

Melena cocked her head. "It's a depiction of my new home."

"You're selling this house? What made you decide to do that?"

Melena told her of the soul searching she'd done since their last conversation and her meeting with the family. "I didn't know until just now what this painting meant, but I've no doubt I'll find that home or the perfect place to build it."

"And that Garrett will be with you in it?"

Melena shrugged. "That I'm not one hundred percent about. But it doesn't matter. This place speaks to my soul."

Pat gathered her into another hug. "Good for you! I'm so proud of you, Mel. How you've grown. As a woman and an artist."

"Speaking of which..." Melena reached for the framed copy of her check that she had yet to hang.

Pat's jaw dropped and eyes widened then she threw back her head and laughed. She turned back to the painting, hemmed and hawed and hummed. "I agree. This place looks, *feels*, like you belong in it. No doubt now that you've put your energy, your creativity into it, it will manifest in your life."

"What do you mean?"

"Through your vision, your painting. Through the desire of your heart. Some call this the law of creation, others the law of attraction. Paul described it best when he said we call those things that be not, as though they are."

Later, after she and Pat visited over lunch and her friend left, Melena sat on her stool, closed her eyes and imagined what it would be like to open that pretty door and walk into the dream cottage she'd depicted on canvas.

Where am I? Who's with me?

I don't know yet, but I'm happy and whole and at peace.

* * * * *

Garrett parked his truck in front of his grandfather's house on the reservation. In the two weeks since he'd left the ranch, he'd stopped more than once on his way to Arizona. Captivated by a photo op—a sunrise, sunset, river or pond. Wildlife and wildflowers. Blue skies, rainbows and thunderclouds. Every day nature spoke to him in a language only fellow travelers on a similar journey would understand. Other than a handful of texts or conversations, he'd hardly spoken to Melena. Sometimes because he was caught up in the moment. Mostly because the place he found himself in had little or no signal. Time to change that. He punched the speed dial button for her number.

"Hey!" His pulse scrambled at the exuberance in her voice.

"Hi yourself."

"Long time, no talk. Everything okay with you?"

"Yeah. Got a ton of photos. You?"

She laughed. "Been working myself. Some. The kids are getting ready for Christmas and all the hoopla is making them, and me, crazy."

"Not in the Christmas spirit?"

"Not really."

He cringed at the sadness in her voice. *Wish I could take it from you, pretty lady.* Garrett hated that he couldn't. This path, this journey, was one only she could take. But he'd be there for her. "You heard from Anne about the week between Christmas and New Years?"

"Yes, she called me yesterday and invited the whole family, even mom and dad."

"Y'all gonna be there?"

"I think so. Kid's haven't fully committed yet, but I'll be there. You?"

"You bet'cha. Especially now." His voice lowered a notch. "Can't wait to see you again."

"Me too."

His heart danced at the lighter tone in her words.

"Pat's home. She may come too."

"Great! It'll be nice to see her."

Melena laughed. They talked a few more minutes, then rang off.

Garrett climbed out of his truck and made his way into the house. His grandfather embraced him.

"Good to see you. You look healthy. Happy."

"I am. More than I ever dreamed I'd be. Or thought I deserved."

"We all deserve happiness. It is the desire of the Great Spirit that we be so. I'm glad you are realizing that for yourself. And allowing it. Your woman, she is okay?"

Garrett didn't have to ask how his grandfather knew about Melena. His grandfather knew about a lot of things. Always had. Something he came to appreciate more as he grew and developed his own intuitive powers. "Yes. Still going through a lot of sadness and grief though. Wish I could make things easier for her."

"She needs more time, but not too much. You have big future together."

Garrett smiled and hugged the old chief hard. "Thanks, Grandfather."

The old man chuckled, winced, sighed. "The Great Spirit call me home soon. You bury me in the tradition of our people, then leave and don't look back. There is nothing here for you after I go."

Garrett swallowed the fears and the protests. It did no good to argue with an elder. Especially the chief—Grandfather or not. Life is a cycle and his grandfather's had run its course. "What about the Shaman? How is he? Who will take over when the Great Spirit calls him home?"

"That is for him to decide. But it won't be you."

"I thought that's what this ability I have was meant for. What I've been trained and groomed to do."

"Your gift may be called upon to help heal some, but not as Shaman. Or chief. You need to run free like the deer and other wild creatures you are so fond of picturing. Promise."

He promised.

Chapter Twenty-One

Garrett paced the lawn in front of the lodge. He'd walked miles so far, waiting for Melena to get to the ranch. He'd arrived yesterday and visited with his cousin, and with Kidd and Marcey and her children. And with the little one on the way. Although he hadn't let them know about her. Better they find out the natural way. He'd talked with Melena nearly every day since he got to the reservation. But now he wanted to see her. Touch her. Hold her. *If that were even possible with her entire family around.*

Frustration swelled at the thought. He'd find a way, make a way, to be alone with her. Even if only for an hour. He closed his eyes, calmed his mind, opened his spirit and sensed her approach. Going to the door, he forced himself to enter the lodge, get a glass of water and sit at a table. His smile welcomed Anne when she pulled out a chair beside him.

"She's close."

Garrett nodded. "Yeah. I feel her too."

"Going to meet the whole family. You okay with that?"

He shrugged. "Gotta happen sometime."

Anne laughed. "Right. Well, we've got to sit down at some point and discuss your upcoming shows."

"I want to be with her."

"I know, and I'll try to make that happen. As much as possible. But you two are in different veins of art. It won't be possible to keep you together for every show."

"I understand that. She still needs time on her own too. But she's new to the art world. Not used to this kind of attention. I don't want her alone in large metropolises."

"Neither do we. Her safety is our utmost concern. Trust me. I'll work it all out. Besides, she's stronger than you think. Or give her credit for."

Garrett winced at the chiding in her tone. Their conversation halted at the jingle of the cowbell on the door. They stood when Melena walked through holding the hand of a little girl that could only be her granddaughter. A smile lit her face when she saw them. Garrett hurried to meet her, took the bag from her shoulder, caressed her cheek with his lips. "Good to see you."

"You too."

He glanced down. "And who might this be?"

"This," Melena urged the child forward, "is Karyn."

Garrett squatted eye-level with the girl. She kept her gaze lowered. A rosy hue covered her creamy cheeks. He took her hand, lifted it to his lips, kissed the back. "Nice to meet you Miss…?"

"Sullivan," Melena supplied. "Kathryn's daughter and my angel girl."

"Miss Sullivan."

Her eyes lifted to meet his. Her giggle shot straight to his heart. He tumbled into love right on the spot. Garrett smiled up at Melena. "You've just been replaced."

Her laughter rang throughout the dining area, danced along his senses. Garrett stood and cradled her cheek in his hand. A subtle shift and nearly imperceptible shake of her head was his cue to back off.

This was not the time and place for the kind of kiss he wanted.

The bell sounded again and the rest of her family and Pat filed into the room.

Garrett hugged Pat then turned to Jon and offered his hand. "Great to see you again."

Jon shook his hand. "Likewise. This is my wife, Deborah."

Garrett tipped his hat. "Nice to meet you, ma'am. And who might this handsome fellow be?"

Deborah glowed. "This is Jon the Third, otherwise known as Trey."

Garrett chucked the child's chin, grinned at the huge belly laugh he received in return and took the boy from his mother at Trey's open-arm invitation. His green eyes sparkled. Gibberish flowed from his little mouth. Garrett gave him his undivided attention, answered with complete solemnity. When their exchange concluded, he handed the baby back to Deborah and turned to Kathryn.

"So glad y'all could come."

She smiled. "Nice of Anne to invite the whole family. This is my husband Chris, and Annabelle."

Garrett accepted Chris's handshake, felt the strength in his grip and noted the sorrow in his gaze. *Strong but tender. Still grieves deeply.* He smiled in understanding, released Chris's hand then squatted to Annabelle's level. "Another pretty little lady. Look more like a Tinkerbelle than an Annabelle."

She giggled, nodded. "I are Tinkerbelle."

"How did you know that's her nickname?" Melena asked.

Garrett grinned up at her. "A hunch."

He stood and reached for Melena's mother's hand, lifted it to his lips and addressed her as he would an elder or wise woman of his tribe. "Hello, grandmother."

An array of emotions lit her eyes. *Sadness. Grief. Hope. Joy.* Garrett held her gaze steady until her lips curved into a welcoming smile.

"Lila Reynolds. Nice to meet you. This is my husband, Sam."

Garrett shook hands with Sam then ushered them farther into the dining area. "We'll get your luggage later. Let's sit and grab a drink."

Before the week ended, Garrett laughed, loved and played more than he had in his entire life. And relished every moment. At fifty, he'd figured his chance to have a family of his own had long since passed. Now he was sure that assumption was totally off. Granted, he may never have a child of his flesh, but he could be a grandfather. One who loved, guided, protected and challenged. Like his had done for him. A quick tug of sorrow pierced him as his grandfather's prediction of the Great Spirit calling him home soon echoed in his mind.

When the New Year had been rung in and everyone was ready to head back to Mississippi, he helped load suitcases and buckle children, then waved goodbye with Melena at his side. He waited until the van was out of sight then turned to her, smoothed his thumbs across her cheeks and lowered his lips to hers in a thorough embrace. He ended the kiss when neither of them could scarcely breathe.

"I've ached to do that all frigging week," he whispered against her mouth.

Melena's laugh shredded the frustration he'd wrestled with since she and her family arrived. He hugged her. "I'm glad you and Pat decided to stay a few more days."

Before she could answer or he could whisk her away to his cabin in town, the lodge door opened. Anne rushed out, sorrow etched in every plane of her face. Garrett's heart twisted. His spirit wrenched then soared in exquisite release.

Grandfather.

"What is it?" Melena's panicked voice broke through the experience.

"Chief Whitecloud, Garrett's grandfather and my uncle, just passed away."

"Oh, no."

"We'll head out within the hour," Garrett told Anne. She nodded and returned to the lodge. He took Melena's hand, led her to his truck. "Come with me while I pack a bag."

Melena sat in silence while Garrett drove to his cabin in town. "I'll make some tea."

He acknowledged her offer with a slight nod. His mind whirled. His spirit wept. He fumbled with the chest that housed his Native American attire. He pulled out the clothing he'd need, buried his face in the soft furs. *Have I thanked you enough? Honored you enough? Loved and respected you enough? Despite that I'm half white, you never turned your back on me. Even when my own father did. I love you, Grandfather. I wanted you to meet her. How will I go on without you?*

"Garrett?" Melena's voice broke through the frantic chatter. Her hand on his shoulder brought instant peace.

He gazed up at her. "Come with me."

Her eyes widened. "What?"

He scrambled to his feet and cupped her head in his hand. "I need you with me. I never thought I'd say that to anyone, never imagined I'd meet someone I could trust or feel safe enough to be vulnerable with."

The quick spurt of concern in her eyes and slight, hesitant shift reminded him she hadn't come to the ranch alone. "Pat can come too if you wish."

The devastation in his azure gaze quelled any arguments Melena may have uttered. There was no real reason she couldn't go. She'd never been to a Reservation or Native American ceremony of any sort. And, luckily, she'd done her laundry yesterday so that wouldn't hold them up. "Okay. I'll text Pat and see if she wants to tag along. Tea's ready."

"Thank you," he whispered then lowered his lips to hers in a kiss so sweet, so full of longing her knees buckled. She clung to him a moment then extricated herself with a shaky breath.

Will I ever get used to the way his kiss makes me feel?

Garrett followed her into the kitchen, sipped the tea then took the mug back with him into the bedroom to finish packing. Melena texted Pat whose enthusiastic response nearly made her laugh. Though a solemn occasion, neither could stop the quick thrill of experiencing the unfamiliar.

Chapter Twenty-Two

Conversation mingled with long stretches of silence accompanied them on the ride to Arizona. Garrett and Anne shared stories of their childhood. Melena and Pat learned how Garrett's father had hated his heritage and when Garrett showed the slightest propensity for Native American culture, he'd tried to beat it out of him. When his sister was born, Garrett's father took him to the reservation and dropped him off. He didn't want her influenced by Garrett or anything Native American.

Garrett was ten at the time and, although his mother had done her best to stay in touch, Garrett didn't see her or his sister until he'd become a man. By then, Angelina—Little Dove, as Garrett called her—was a teenager and curious. She'd asked more than once for Garrett to take her to the reservation with him. She hated their father, was afraid of him. As it turned out, she'd had every right to be both. She was only sixteen when she and their mother died.

"What made you go into law enforcement?" Melena asked during one of the breaks in conversation. "Especially with your talent in photography?"

"At first I wanted to be on the Tribal Council to be an advocate for the rights of children of mixed races. I started college for a degree in Criminal Justice. One day I did a ride-along with the Arizona State Police and I was hooked. My instinct and intuition became valuable assets and I worked my way up the ranks very quickly. I became a detective, then DEA agent. From there I moved into the CIA."

"And the rest, as they say, is history." Anne touched his shoulder, smiled at Melena and Pat. That conversation ended in unspoken but mutual consent.

"Tell us about your grandfather," Pat encouraged.

Garrett told of how his grandfather had struggled a long time to understand his son. Disappointed in the way Garrett's dad turned out, he'd done his best to guide and protect Garrett from becoming jaded against his natural abilities while allowing him the room to grow as both a Native American and a white man. "He told me last time I visited a couple of weeks ago that the Great Spirit would be calling him home. I just didn't expect it so soon."

"Really?" Anne asked.

Garrett nodded. "Yeah, he's always been enigmatic, said things I didn't fully understand, many of which I comprehended later. One thing I haven't figured out yet is a comment he made about my gift making room for me."

"Strange..." Anne remarked.

"What's so strange about it?" Pat asked.

Garrett shrugged. "I just don't know what he meant. We were talking about my reveal at the art show and he said my gift had made room for me."

"Proverbs 16:6," Pat said. "A man's gift makes room for him and brings him before great men."

"Aaahh, that's what he meant when he said for me to search my great book!"

"So your grandfather studied the Bible too?"

Garrett smiled. "Seems that way." *You sly, old fox.*

They arrived at the reservation in less time than Garrett had ever made the trip alone. Switching drivers every four or five hours made the trek less arduous on everyone. Garrett met with the Shaman and set up arrangements for his grandfather's burial according to the tribe's ancestral traditions. He performed the cleansing ritual and stayed with the Chief throughout the following days. Anne, Melena and Pat were whisked away by women elders and participated in their own purification ceremonies before they were allowed to attend the wake.

Melena had never seen, heard or experienced a more wrenching yet exquisite funeral. Accompanied by drums, the songs, chants, and prayers touched her in a way nothing else had. The sight of Garrett in his garments, paint on his face, the rich tone of his voice and haunting cry in his tone as he mourned, dancing and singing, spoke volumes to her. Showed her his depths far better than any time they'd spent together to date.

She absorbed each sight, sound, emotion, and envisioned them on canvas and in glass. One day she'd recreate the experience, careful not to identify the tribe or its members, nor show disrespect in any manner. Less than a week later, they returned to the ranch, exhausted but at peace. She and Pat stayed an extra two days to recoup from the trip, then left for Mississippi.

* * * * *

One year later Melena stood looking out of the entrance of her new home. So much had transpired in the last twelve months she could hardly absorb it all. After Garrett's grandfather's funeral, she returned to work at the ranch during the retreat. Missy had indeed earned the scholarship to attend and had a wonderful time—so much so that she'd moved there permanently to work and develop her art. Her boyfriend came with her and was employed as a wrangler and maintenance man.

She and Garrett embarked on their individual as well as combined or multi-genre tours with fellow Crossed Penn artists. Anne had scheduled the events in various cities, large and small, beginning with Melena's home state. While out exploring the countryside on one of her "inspirational ramblings," she'd spotted her cottage.

Located less than two hours from her hometown, the architecture matched the chalet in her painting brick for brick. The only differences were in the colors of the doors and trim work. She'd changed those immediately.

Packing up her home of nearly thirty years hadn't been easy, but now that it was all done and she was settled in, Melena knew she'd made the best possible decision for herself and her future. She still missed Jon and found she carried little pellets of grief that occasionally exploded into a full-blown episode. Just as intense as when he died, but thankfully not as often.

Still hard to believe he's been gone more than two years. Sometimes it feels like yesterday, at others—an eternity.

Inhaling, she drew in the scents of Sweet Pea, Jasmine and other winter-flowering plants blooming in her yard. She smiled to herself and welcomed the thrill of accomplishment, ownership and independence that flowed through her.

Thank You, God, for all of my blessings. For this lovely home, my life with Jon and my life now. By Your grace, I've grown so much.

So have the kids and grandkids. Everyone is doing so well and although we miss him every day, I'm grateful for the good plan, the future and the hope You have for me, for us, in this New Year.

Pleasant sensations scurried up her spine. Melena closed her eyes, waited, and barely flinched when Garrett's arms slipped around her waist. She tilted her face for his kiss.

"How does it feel now that you're all done with moving?"

"Like I'm right where I'm supposed to be." She turned, slid her hands up his back and rested her cheek against his heart. "Right where I want to be."

Dear Readers,

If you've known me for long, you know I lost my beloved husband in 2009 and by God's grace, lived and worked at the Silver Spur Guest Ranch in Bandera from 2010 - 2014. *My Heart Weeps* is a rendition of my journey from wife to widow to individual. Although Melena's situation parallels mine, for the sake of brevity and to spare you from the harsh realities of how debilitating grief can be, I shortened her grieving/healing process.

Alas, grief can linger for years and is personal to the individual. We, as family, friends, and loved ones of those grieving must do our best to understand and accept the choices they make, even when we don't agree or feel we know better. One the best ways to do this is through prayer, asking God to give you an understanding heart.

Grief truly is, as Melena puts it, "the valley of the shadow of death." It can incapacitate you completely until you have no idea of your life purpose, what you're here for, or even if you should continue to live.

Don't give up! Don't stay stuck in that awful place.

God promises in Jeremiah 29:11 that He has a great plan, a future and hope for you, if only you believe. If only you trust. Take Him at His word and walk through the valley onto the mountaintop of His blessings.

If you don't know Him already, I pray you seek a closer walk with the Lord, for only He can pull you through the tough times in your life. And remember, He is with you in every valley and on every mountaintop.

Pamela S Thibodeaux
"Inspirational with an Edge!" ™

About the Author

Pamela S. Thibodeaux grew up in the town of Iowa, Louisiana. She is the mother of four (two by blood and two by marriage) and a grandmother. A deeply committed Christian, Pamela firmly believes in God and His promises.

"God is very real to me, and I feel people today need and want to hear more of His truths wherever they can glean them. People are hungry for practical (and real) Christian values, not some 'holier-than-thou' beliefs which are impossible to believe and impossible to live up to," Pamela says. "I do my best to encourage readers to develop a personal relationship with God. The deepest desire of my heart is to glorify God and to get His message of faith, trust, and forgiveness to a hurting world."

Email Pamela at: **pam@pamelathibodeaux.com**
Visit her website: **https://www.pamelathibodeaux.com/**
Or blog: **http://pamswildroseblog.blogspot.com**

Other Titles by Pamela S. Thibodeaux

Love's Overcoming Power

Temptation, Abuse, Grief and Doubt are plagues common to women all over the world. In John, 16 Jesus said.... In the world you will have tribulation but be of good cheer, for I have overcome the world.

In this Women's Fiction collection comprised of three full-length novels and one novella, Pamela S Thibodeaux shares stories that exemplify the power of God's love to overcome whatever situations life throws at you.

Includes: ***The Visionary, Circles of Fate, My Heart Weeps*** and ***Keri's Christmas Wish.***

Keri's Christmas Wish

For as long as she can remember, Keri Jackson has despised the hype and commercialism around Christmas so much she seldom enjoys the holiday. Will she get her wish and be free of the angst to truly enjoy Christmas this year?

A devout Christian at heart, Jeremy Hinton, a Psychotherapist, Life Coach, Spiritual Mentor and Energy Medicine Practitioner has studied all of the world's religions and homeopathic healing modalities. But when a rare bacterial infection threatens the life of the woman he loves, will all of his faith and training be for naught?

Circles of Fate

Set at the tail end of the Vietnam War era, **Circles of Fate** takes the reader from Fort Benning, Georgia to Thibodaux, Louisiana. A romantic saga, this gripping novel covers nearly twenty years in the lives of Shaunna Chatman and Todd Jameson. Constantly thrown together and torn apart by fate, the two are repeatedly forced to choose between love and duty, right and wrong, standing on faith or succumbing to the world's viewpoint on life, love, marriage and fidelity. With intriguing twists and turns, fate brings together a cast of characters whose lives will forever be entwined. Through it all is the hand of God as He works all things together for the good of those who love Him and are called according to His purpose.

The Visionary ~ Where the awesome power of God's love heals the most wounded of souls...

A visionary is someone who sees into the future Taylor Forrestier sees into the past but only as it pertains to her work. Hailed by her peers as *"a visionary with an instinct for beauty and an eye for the unique"* Taylor is undoubtedly a brilliant architect and gifted designer. But she and twin brother Trevor, share more than a successful business. The two share a childhood wrought with lies and deceit and the kind of abuse that's disgustingly prevalent in today's society. Can the love of God and the awesome healing power of His grace and mercy free the twins from their past and open their hearts to the good plan and the future He has for their lives?

Love is a Rose **(devotional)**

Music is the magical entry into the spirit world; the golden gate into the Kingdom of God. But we mustn't be of the mindset that God only uses Christian music to reach out and touch our mind, heart, and spirit. God uses any and **every** means available to speak to His children.

Our job is to be open and receptive.

In this devotional, Pamela S Thibodeaux shares how God opened her spirit to a deeper understanding of the abundance of His grace and mercy through the words of the song, The Rose sung by Country & Western artist Conway Twitty.

Pamela offers Seeds to Ponder and a prayer as she parallels the love of God and the Christian life to each verse of the song.

The Tempered Series Collection

Start at the beginning and follow these beloved characters throughout the years as love crosses the lines of age and strengthens the bonds of friendship. Contains: ***Tempered Hearts, Tempered Dreams, Tempered Fire, Tempered Joy, Lori's Redemption***

Tempered Hearts (book 1 in Tempered series)

Rancher Craig Harris and veterinarian Tamera Collins clash from the moment they meet. Innocence is pitted against arrogance as tempers rise and passions ignite to form a love as pure as the finest gold, fresh from the crucible and as strong as steel. Thrown together amid tragedy and unsated passion, Tamera and Craig share a strong attraction that neither accepts as the first stages of love. Torn between desire and dislike, they must make peace with their pasts and God in order to open up to the love blossoming between them. It is a love that nothing can destroy when they come to understand that **only when hearts are tempered, minds are opened, and wills are softened can man discern the will of God for his life.**

Tempered Dreams (book 2 in Tempered Series)

Dr. Scott Hensley (introduced in Tempered Hearts) has built a wall around his heart since the death of his wife and parents. Katrina Simmons is recovering from scars inflicted on her as a battered wife. Can dreams be renewed and faith strengthened? Can they find joy and peace in God's love and in love for one another?

Tempered Fire (book 3 in Tempered Series)

Amber Harris is a good girl on the brink of womanhood. Stanley Morrison is a young man at the start of his life. For each other, they have always felt the fireworks that two people in love should feel. But the questions about his past, his pride, and Amber's father might be the end of what could be a strong relationship. As the two try to protect their budding romance, some unlikely but powerful forces conspire to keep them apart. Will they survive the wishes of everyone around them with their relationship intact?

Tempered Joy (book 4 in Tempered series)

All around rodeo cowboy and heir to the Rockin' H Ranch, Ace Harris is determined not to fall in love. He's only loved one woman in his life, his mother, and no one can even come close to filling her boots. Lexie Morgan thinks rodeo cowboys have rocks for brains and a death wish for a soul. A broken childhood and the death of her father and best friend leave her doubting and questioning God (despite her years of religious upbringing) and afraid of love. Can two young people who clash from the onset learn to trust in the healing power of God and find love and happiness amidst tragedy and grief?

Lori's Redemption

Lori Strickland (introduced in *Tempered Fire*) has always been known as her father's "wild child" with no desire to change until she meets ex-bull-rider-turned-preacher, Rafe Judson. Her attempts to change her wanton ways come to naught until she realizes redemption only comes with true repentance. Can she find redemption and win the heart of the cowboy preacher?

Tempered Truth (book 5 in the Tempered Series)

Fate declared them neighbors. Scandal insisted they were brothers. The fact that they looked enough alike to be twins only added fuel to the rumors flying about their parentage.

For fifty-plus years Craig Harris and Scott Hensley have enjoyed a bond nothing can sever.

Not the insinuations that they share the same father.

Not the years of strife and grief and heartache.

Not even death.

Will the truth set them free, or will it destroy the friendship that has lasted a lifetime?

The Inheritance

The Inheritance is about the chance we all long for...the chance to start over. Widowed at age thirty-nine and suffering from empty nest syndrome, Rebecca Sinclair is overshadowed by grief and loneliness. Her husband has been deceased for a year, her oldest child has moved to New York in pursuit of an acting career and her youngest child is attending college in France. Having spent over half of her life as a wife and mother, she has no idea what God has in store for her now. Will an unexpected inheritance in the wine country of New York bring meaning and purpose to her life and give her the courage to love again?

 US Postal worker Raymond Jacobey has been in love with the little widow since he first set eyes on her. A wanderer searching for the ever-elusive soul mate, Ray has never stayed in one place too long. Raised by self-centered, high-power executives, he's longed for the idyllic life of residing in a cozy house in a small town with the love of his life. Will he gain the heart of the lovely widow, or will he lose her to the wine country of New York?

Anytime is the perfect time for love.

In ***Love in Season***, author Pamela S Thibodeaux brings together eight of her most beloved romance stories—one for each season plus four holidays that revolve around love and family. Includes (Winter) **Winter Madness**, (Valentine's Day) **Choices**, (Spring) **Cathy's Angel**, (Easter) **Lilies for Sandi** (NEW), (Summer) **The Big Catch** (NEW), (Fall) **A Hero for Jessica**, (Thanksgiving) **Review of Love** (NEW) and (Christmas) **In His Sight**.

Sienna has survived what most succumb to - the death of a spouse and child and has maintained her faith despite her troubles. William has never met anyone who actually lived out what they say they believe. Is it true love between the faithful optimist and broody pessimist or simply ***Winter Madness***? *Part of **Love in Season** collection of short stories*

Best-selling novelist and songwriter, Camie Rogers has penned numerous accounts of the secret love she holds in her heart. Country-Music Superstar Kip Allen has changed from the shy, humble boy, to the epitome of "star." Can the two rediscover each other after one night of his Home is Where the Heart is Tour? Find out in ***Choices*** *Part of **Love in Season** collection of short stories*

Single mom Cathy Johnson is tired of running her life alone...what she needs is a well-trained angel to help out. Jared Savoy gave up the dream of having a family when he discovered he is sterile. Can a confirmed bachelor and the mother of four find love amid normal daily chaos? Find out in **Cathy's Angel** *Part of **Love in Season** collection of short stories*

Sandi and Brett did everything backwards. They got pregnant before the wedding and had a baby instead of a honeymoon. Since, Brett has resented the fact that his dreams of a football career have been cut short and wonders how long it'll take God to forgive him for his mistakes. Sandi has played second fiddle to Brett's dreams and desires to the point of not knowing herself any longer and fears her marriage will never be a true one because of their failures. Can two hearts broken by unfulfilled dreams find healing, wholeness, and restoration? Find out in **Lilies for Sandi** *Part of **Love in Season** collection of short stories*

Karla and, the love of her life, Jeff, have uncovered some uncommon ground: The Great Outdoors. For the life of her, she does not understand his love of fishing and how he can spend so much time doing so. Will she come to love the sport as much as he or will his passion for a rod and reel tangle up their relationship? Find out in **The Big Catch** *Part of **Love in Season** collection of short stories*

Anthony Paul Seville is known as the 'most eligible bachelor' in New Orleans, possibly even the entire state of Louisiana, but finds himself alone—completely and explicitly alone. Jessica Aucoin is a writer on her way to fame and fortune but is haunted by a man from her past. Will the "champion" lawyer and the author of romantic suspense find love written in their future? Find out in ***A Hero for Jessica*** *Part of **Love in Season** collection of short stories*

Jason Stockwell has been commissioned to interview Kylie Erickson and to review her books. Only problem is, she won't give the time of day much less an interview to someone whose type of writing she deems not worthy of respect. Can they suspend their judgmental attitudes and find true love? Find out in ***Review of Love*** *Part of **Love in Season** collection of short stories*

Grade-school teacher Carson Alexander has a gift—a gift that has driven a wedge between him and his family. Worse, it's put him at odds with God. Feeling alone and misunderstood, Carson views God's gift of prophecy as the worst kind of curse...that is until he meets Lorelei Conner, landscape artist extraordinaire, and perhaps the one person who may need Carson and his gift more than anyone ever has.

Lorelei Connor is a mother on the run. Her abusive ex-husband has followed her all over the country trying to steal their daughter. Distrusting of men and needing to keep on the move, she's surprised by her desire to remain close to Carson Alexander. Through her fear and hesitation, she must learn to rely on God to guide her—not an easy task when He's prompting her to trust a man. Can their relationship withstand the tragedy lurking on the horizon? Find out in *In His Sight* *Part of **Love in Season** collection of short stories*

**Temperance
Publishing**